Remy stopped the car at the dead end of a deserted road. "I didn't think you were ready to go back yet," he said.

Susan drew a slow, deep breath and turned to him. "I wasn't," she whispered, feeling his unwavering gaze on her.

Remy reached for her as she leaned toward him. His mouth was hot fire on hers, and she drew its heat to her, pressing her body against his muscular length. Whatever concerns she might have had about him faded in his arms. If she was being a fool, she didn't care—but she knew she wasn't. She'd found the core of honor in this man, and it was enough for her.

Remy began to unbutton the top of her white linen dress, and his hands brushed her bare skin. "You feel like satin," he said quietly. His eyes were glazed with passion as he seared her with one glance, then branded the pale, soft skin of her throat with his mouth. He tasted her endlessly until she could bear it no longer and pulled his mouth up to hers again, giving him her passion and absorbing his.

After a few moments Remy pulled away. "You'll be the death of me, cher."

Susan laughed contentedly. "My grandmother will probably kill us both."

"It would be worth it."

"Do you think we're too old to be necking in a car like teenagers?" she asked.

Remy grinned. "Not a chance. . . ."

WHAT ARE *LOVESWEPT* ROMANCES?

They are stories of true romance and touching emotion. We believe those two very important ingredients are constants in our highly sensual and very believable stories in the *LOVESWEPT* line. Our goal is to give you, the reader, stories of consistently high quality that may sometimes make you laugh, sometimes make you cry, but are always fresh and creative and contain many delightful surprises within their pages.

Most romance fans read an enormous number of books. Those they truly love, they keep. Others may be traded with friends and soon forgotten. We hope that each *LOVESWEPT* romance will be a treasure—a "keeper." We will always try to publish

LOVE STORIES YOU'LL NEVER FORGET
BY AUTHORS YOU'LL ALWAYS REMEMBER

The Editors

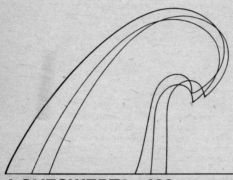

LOVESWEPT® • 403

Linda Cajio
Just One Look

 BANTAM BOOKS
NEW YORK • TORONTO • LONDON • SYDNEY • AUCKLAND

JUST ONE LOOK

A Bantam Book / June 1990

LOVESWEPT® and the wave device are registered
trademarks of Bantam Books, a division of
Bantam Doubleday Dell Publishing Group, Inc.
Registered in U.S. Patent
and Trademark Office and elsewhere.

If you would be interested in receiving protective vinyl
covers for your Loveswept books, please write to this address
for information:

Loveswept
Bantam Books
P.O. Box 985
Hicksville, NY 11802

ISBN 0-553-44034-9

Published simultaneously in the United States and Canada

Bantam Books are published by Bantam Books, a division
of Bantam Doubleday Dell Publishing Group, Inc. Its trademark, consisting of the words "Bantam Books" and the
portrayal of a rooster, is Registered in U.S. Patent and
Trademark Office and in other countries. Marca Registrada.
Bantam Books, 666 Fifth Avenue, New York, New York 10103.

PRINTED IN THE UNITED STATES OF AMERICA

OPM   0 9 8 7 6 5 4 3 2 1

*For Cutie, who was loved by all and is still sorely missed by many.
With much love. L.*

One

He watched her.

He was being paid to watch her, but that didn't mean he couldn't enjoy the view. A man had few pleasures in his line of work. Susan Kitteridge was proving to be one of them.

The droning voices of the sunbathers combined with the heat should have been lulling, but they weren't. He didn't need the raucous calls of the sea gulls to keep him from nodding off. The woman was too intriguing, not at all what he'd expected.

As he pulled his baseball cap lower on his forehead and settled back against the wooden bench, he decided she didn't look like spy material. Still, no one ever really did. That was the beauty of it.

She was lying on the beach almost directly below him. He was admiring the tapering line of her back when she flipped over to expose her front to the sun.

The world stopped.

Her features were beautiful, exotic. He surveyed, with pleasure, her high cheekbones, winged eyebrows, and the long lashes shadowing her smooth skin. Her mouth was lush in repose, tempting a man to taste the passion that must lie just beneath the surface. Her breasts were full, and her bandeau top made him wonder when it would give way and bare tight nipples to his sight. "If" was not the operative word on the bathing suit. The sucker was going to give at any moment. Her waist, in contrast to her breasts, was taut, her belly supple before her body curved into hips that could only lead a man beyond redemption. And how he wanted to sin.

But what left him gaping was the way her slender thighs were parted slightly, as though to trap the sun's rays between them. He could almost feel the heat caressing her satiny flesh, warming it. Sweat that had nothing to do with the day's heat broke out on his forehead.

Too bad she was so beautiful.

Too bad she was a traitor.

Too bad she was his assignment.

"Really, Susan, that bathing suit looks about ready to fall off you at any moment."

"You're no fun, Grandmother," Susan Kitteridge said as she stood up. The top dipped dangerously low, exposing creamy skin. She yanked it up again, grinning at her grandmother. Lettice Kitteridge glared back. She was dressed in a one-piece suit, and an ankle-length terry cover, *and* a large straw hat and sunglasses. She was also sitting inside a canvas cabana. She must just like the sea air, Susan decided. Or else Lettice was really Vampira out for a day's jaunt.

Her grandmother's glare was piercing in spite

of the sunglasses. Susan sighed. Maybe Lettice had a point. The suit did seem a bit small. She slipped on a wrinkled gauze shirt. Leaving it unbuttoned, she tied the tails together at her waist, then turned around for her grandmother's inspection. "This way if the top falls off, I'm still covered."

"In a pig's eye!" Lettice exclaimed, shaking her head.

"It could be worse, Grandmother. It could have fallen off already."

"I'm grateful for small things." Lettice glanced at her watch. "Almost four. About ready to go home, dear?"

"Yes. And you've had enough sun, I'm sure," Susan said, chuckling. She wrapped a sarong around herself, tying it at her waist.

As she helped her grandmother pick up their beach things, she couldn't keep her hands from trembling. Somehow she had managed yet again to hide from her grandmother the turmoil inside herself. She had automatically slipped into her party-girl image, as if it were a second skin. It was so easy, too easy, after all her years of practice. But now, in the aftermath, she was sick and shaken.

Susan clamped her teeth together to hold back the scream that threatened to erupt. How could she act normal when everything she believed in was being turned inside out? She knew what she should do, but she didn't know if she could do it. She couldn't turn her back on a long friendship, but she couldn't turn her back on what she had seen either.

She forced the memory out of her mind. For weeks she had been haunted by it. She couldn't live with herself now, and no matter what course of action she picked, she didn't know if she could live with herself afterward.

She felt as if she had lost the real Susan Kitteridge somewhere, and so two weeks earlier she had left Washington and everything behind her and come home to family. Oddly enough, not to her parents or her reclusive brother, Rick, who were all living in England. She had returned to her grandmother, Lettice Kitteridge, the matriarch of one of Philadelphia's first families. Lettice had never been a "let's bake cookies" grandmother. Susan almost laughed out loud at the thought. But she needed a dose of her grandmother's common sense and indomitable spirit. Lettice, who had left her Gladwynne, Pennsylvania, mansion for her shore house in Ventnor City, New Jersey, to arrange a charity affair there, had welcomed her granddaughter with open arms—and a lecture for being obsessed with the Washington, D.C., party circuit.

If only Lettice knew what her granddaughter actually was . . .

"Don't forget the basket," Lettice said, interrupting Susan's thoughts.

Susan smiled to herself. Here she was, wrestling with a scandal that would rock Washington to its toes, and her grandmother was telling her the most mundane of things. It was a cockeyed perspective, but a perspective just the same.

"Bless you, Grandmother," she murmured. "I won't."

She put on her Phillies baseball cap, then picked up the basket and followed Lettice off the beach.

Remy St. Jacques sauntered behind the two women, careful to keep a respectable distance from them.

He knew the woman with Susan Kitteridge was her grandmother, even though she was covered from head to toe. One tough old lady by all reports. Remy smiled when the women turned toward one of the walkways off the boardwalk. The direction they were taking made it clear they were heading back to the grandmother's summer house, six blocks away. A castle was more like it, he thought, picturing the huge old Victorian place in his mind. His room at the Sea Drift motel, while clean and livable, was a far cry from the Kitteridge mansion. Technically he should be admiring Susan's audacity in using her own grandmother as a cover for her operations. Instead, he was disgusted by it.

"You're losing your edge, *cher*," he muttered to himself.

He wondered if he had already lost it. Ten years in the Company's internal affairs section was bound to make anyone lose his edge. One saw things when investigating "turned" agents. One did things . . .

He forced the thoughts away. He had a job to do. One last job, and then he would tell Ross Mitchelson it was over. No more. He was tired and burnt out. That was bad for someone in his occupation. Very bad.

As he kept pace behind them, he gazed at Susan's dark hair. It was pulled back in a ponytail that hung to her shoulders. He had never seen hair so rich in color that it was nearly black. Her filmy shirt enticed rather than hid, as did the long skirt that exposed one leg to view as she walked. Very sexy, he thought. Extremely sexy. And in the midst of extremely sexy was a maroon baseball cap pulled low across her brow. Somehow she made it work with the rest of the outfit. At least her cap looked a helluva lot better on her than his ever would.

He truly didn't understand why she was doing what she was doing. She came from a prestigious family, and she exuded sophistication and self-confidence with every movement. Her father, the old lady's son, had even been an ambassador to the Court of St. James's. She had married an up and coming diplomat, Richard Ames. But after he had died, Susan had taken back her maiden name and become a courier for the Company. She used a Washington party girl cover, and Ross said she was very good at retrieving and passing along incoming data.

Now she was about to sell sensitive documents to an unfriendly government.

He slowed as Susan and her grandmother stopped at a small, exclusive boutique called Pearls and Lace. They went inside, and Remy casually strolled up to the window to admire the intimate apparel display. Lace teddies, satin nightgowns, and silk garters from Marks and Lindley, expensive enough to drain a man's wallet and sexy enough to set his blood on fire, were intermixed with jewelry and other accessories. The display looked as if a woman had draped the lingerie all over her bed in an effort to choose the most alluring.

Through the window Remy saw Susan pick up a pair of turquoise bikini panties. His blood surged heavily in his veins. He wasn't going to survive if he kept having this reaction to her. She had "turned," and that knowledge should kill any desire for her. Ross said she was even part of a new spy network. Remy shook his head. Why was she doing it? For kicks? She certainly didn't act like an ideologist, and she certainly didn't need the money. Not that selling secrets paid all that well.

It just didn't make sense. And he had been pulled off a job to baby-sit Susan, a newly born "mole." That didn't make sense either.

She set down the panties, to his relief. But she didn't move on to another item. Instead, she stared off into space, her expression changing from curiosity to something else. For a long moment her features held a look of unbearable sadness and vulnerability. Then she turned . . . straight toward him.

Remy froze as the unthinkable happened. His quarry gazed straight into his eyes. She smiled and tipped her head in an action of good manners when two strangers catch each other's glances. He could do nothing but smile back in brief acknowledgment. Etiquette done, she walked over to her grandmother.

Every muscle in Remy's body collapsed. He managed to gaze down at the window display with calculated casualness, then saunter off along the street.

Your edge is definitely gone, he thought.

For the first time in his career he'd been spotted.

Susan helped her grandmother out of the car, careful to guide Lettice to the sidewalk in front of the Palace Casino's restaurant.

"Susan," her grandmother said with exaggerated patience. "I'm not some helpless old lady, which you would know if you came home more often."

Susan laughed. "So Ellen and Anne told me. I'm sorry. I just didn't want you to fall."

"Simply pick me up if I do." She patted Susan's cheek. "Now, just what did your cousins tell you?"

"Well . . ." She wasn't sure how much she should say, then decided her grandmother would probably get a chuckle out of it. Susan herself certainly had. "That I was crazy to come down to the shore with you because you probably had some elaborate scheme to fix me up with a man. That you had fixed both of them up, and after those experiences they highly recommended I go to some deserted island or the Canadian backwoods for an extended stay—like the rest of my life."

"What utter nonsense," Lettice proclaimed. "I will admit that I love having great-grandchildren, but I wouldn't fix any of you up willy-nilly. I do it very carefully."

"Grandmother!" Susan was horrified. If Lettice were really up to some matchmaking scheme . . . Please no, Susan thought. It was the last thing she needed.

Lettice patted her arm in reassurance. "Relax, Susan. Do you see a man around?"

"No."

"Then I'm not matchmaking . . . for the moment."

Susan panicked until she caught the amusement in her grandmother's eye. Sighing with relief, she escorted Lettice into the restaurant.

But there had been a man, Susan thought, remembering the incident at Pearls and Lace. Her internal war between loyalty and right had arisen again in the boutique, and when she'd finally got it under control, she had glanced up to see a man gazing at the window display. His face had been shaded by his baseball cap, so that she could make out his features but couldn't see them distinctly. He'd had a lean face, all angles it had seemed, and dark hair. When their eyes met, something had run through her, a kind of shock she couldn't define. Suddenly she had become all too aware of the lingerie she'd held in her hands, and she had wanted him to be aware of it too. That primitive jolt had shaken her, and in spite of the brief look, she knew she would recognize him again.

She decided not to tell her grandmother about the man. She wasn't sure if her cousins or Lettice were serious, but there was no sense taking chances. Anyway, she'd probably never see the man again.

But she did.

She and Lettice had no sooner entered the casino area for a little "excitement," as Lettice called it, when Susan saw him. He was standing by the slot machines, actually leaning on one nonchalantly. She stared at him as she took a seat behind her grandmother at the baccarat table. Baccarat was by reservation only, so only the players and their guests were allowed beyond the ropes.

He hadn't noticed her yet as he surveyed the lower level of the casino. He was taller than she'd thought, and a little older, too, in his mid-thirties. But she hadn't been wrong about the dark hair and the lean, angular face. His hair was a deep coffee color, thick and brushed straight back from his forehead. His features were chiseled in intriguing planes and angles, not too sharp, but certainly not soft. Experience was stamped all over them. Dressed in jeans and a black shirt, he didn't appear to have an ounce of fat anywhere. He was looking unhappy and disgusted, and she wondered if he was waiting for someone who was late. A woman?

Disappointment shot through her, then she realized how silly it was to fantasize about a man she'd only glimpsed through a boutique window. Still, she was grateful for the diversion he provided.

He glanced up, and a wave of heat curled in her stomach and spread outward. She was held captive by a look, just a look, from a man she didn't know. . . .

"I'm gonna beat the pants off this place," Lettice said, shifting around in her chair.

"What?" Susan asked, dragging her gaze from the man to her grandmother.

"I said I'm going to take the house," Lettice repeated, glancing to where Susan had just been looking.

Heat flooding her cheeks, Susan watched as her grandmother gave a long, appraising look at the slot machines—and the man.

A bold move was needed, Susan decided, to divert her grandmother from any notions that her granddaughter needed or wanted a man. Leaning forward, she said in a low voice, "Do you suppose he has the hots for you?"

Lettice arched an eyebrow. "He should be so lucky."

Susan grinned as her grandmother turned back to the game, then breathed a mental sigh of relief at heading Lettice off.

If only the rest of her life were so easy.

Now the old lady had seen him!

Remy cursed under his breath as he thought of the previous night's incident for the hundredth time. He was hanging back an entire half block as he followed the women down the boards, preferring to risk losing them rather than being spotted a third time.

This whole assignment was a mess, he admitted. It had been from the first moment, when an urgent call from Ross had pulled him off his current case. He had been following up a vague rumor that someone in the Company was arranging a deal for a lot of money. He had the "why," but the who, what, when, and where were still missing. Ross wanted to keep Susan Kitteridge very quiet, though, and he had told Remy he needed someone he could absolutely trust. He should have told Ross, Remy thought, that what Ross really needed was to pension off his burnt-out employees, namely Remy St. Jacques. Still, Remy could understand Ross's motives.

So much for very quiet, he thought, shoving his sunglasses back on his nose. He might as well have won the million-dollar slots last night. The result would have been the same.

What the hell was wrong with him? His mental state must be worse than he had imagined. This was supposed to be a simple observation of her, of her habits and daily routine, in an attempt to know her. It was amazing how much people, even trained people, gave away through unconscious habit. Ross had someone on the other side, very high up, who would be able to give him the time and place of Susan's exchange. That was not a problem for once, and Ross only needed someone there when the moment was right.

That was him, Remy. But now he'd been spotted and acknowledged. Ross wouldn't like that.

Well, Remy thought, he had observed her daily routine of lying on the beach and chauffeuring her grandmother somewhere. He had observed the way she could turn him inside out with one look. He had also observed an expression of sadness that surfaced from time to time, making her appear as vulnerable as a young girl. It was hardly the look one expected of someone about to sell out. In fact, it was the exact opposite.

He knew he ought to be calling Ross and telling him to bring in someone else, but some instinct held him back. He'd learned to listen to those instincts. He was listening now to the vague feeling that something was wrong somewhere.

As Susan and her grandmother settled on the beach and he took up his post on a bench, Remy decided a little extra caution on his part could rectify his earlier mistakes.

Yes, being spotted was bad, but it wasn't cause for panic.

He'd been in worse situations. A little caution and a little bayou luck, as his mama would say, and he'd be fine.

Susan looked around the beach, realized what she was doing, and immediately stopped.

Okay, she thought as she gathered up her things for the trek back to the house. So she hadn't seen the sexy man in several days. He had been a nice diversion when she had badly needed one. A person was entitled to lust in her heart upon occasion.

"Got the basket?" Lettice asked.

Susan snatched it up. "Yup."

Lettice insisted on walking to and from the beach for exercise. She was eccentric that way. But today the walk seemed longer than usual, or, Susan decided, she had lost more sleep than usual. She was running out of time before she had to make a decision about Ross Mitchelson. One she hated to make. After all Ross had done for her, she didn't even know if she could. Yet she didn't know how she couldn't.

"I want to stop at that shop just off the board-walk," Lettice said.

Susan nodded in answer.

"You're quiet."

"Tired."

"Well, you better perk up for tonight."

Susan groaned, thinking of the charity night her grandmother had been arranging with the Palace Casino. She had come there to think things through, wanting only the peace and quiet of bak-ing on the beach and watching the sailboats glide across the ocean, not one of her grandmother's grand balls, no matter how worthy the cause.

"Grandmother, I don't think—" Susan began.

Lettice turned around. Being mummified in a sunhat and robe didn't hamper her "regal eye." "You aren't intending to beg off, are you, Susan?"

"Well, I'm very tired, and you don't need me—"

"But I was so looking forward to your being there. You're at every party in Washington, Lord knows why, and you can't even go to one event with your own grandmother?" Lettice paused for a long moment. "I think not, Susan."

She made a face. "You're not going to let me off."

Lettice smiled. "Hardly. The seafood shop is just ahead. I'll buy us a couple of lobsters for Mamie to cook as compensation."

"Then I think I can face the evening," Susan said, deciding she could force herself to struggle through the evening to please her grandmother—and to eat some of Mamie's lobster.

They turned the corner and went inside the tiny shop. When they emerged a short time later, they were loaded with lobster. Overloaded.

Susan struggled to hold basket, beach chair, beach tote, and a plastic bag of two scrabbling lobsters. She was losing the battle and she knew it.

"Don't drop it!" Lettice warned.

"Well, take something!" Susan snapped back.

Her grandmother took the lobster bag and held it at arm's length. "If I get to know it, I won't want to eat it."

"All the more for me," Susan said, straightening.

"Selfish child." Lettice looked around and immediately snagged the first person she saw. It didn't matter that the man was going in the opposite direction, back toward the corner. She touched his arm and pulled him around.

"Well, hello there. I was wondering if you could help my granddaughter and me carry a few things. We live just up the street."

Without waiting for an answer, Lettice thrust the bag into the man's hands.

Susan gasped. It wasn't just any man Lettice was giving the lobster treatment to.

It was *her* sexy man.

Two

Frozen, Remy stared at the bag he now held, the lobsters inside desperately scrambling to escape their doom.

He knew exactly how the creatures felt.

"Lovely," Lettice Kitteridge said, seeming to think his one mission in life was to help her. "You're one of the few gentlemen left in the world, young man. Now, if you'll just take a few things from my granddaughter . . ."

Remy sighed. "Of course."

They never covered this in the training course at Langley, he thought as he helplessly took the beach chair and basket from Susan. She looked as shocked as he felt.

As the three of them set off down the street, he smothered rising curses while wondering what the hell else he could have done. He had come around the corner just in time to see them in front of the shop and *not* halfway down the street where, according to his calculations, they should have been. He had immediately turned back to avoid the disaster of being spotted again. Instead, he'd been roped into service. He would have to assess the damage later, though. Right now he had to concentrate on just being an innocent Good Samaritan.

"I'm Lettice Kitteridge," the older woman said.

"Remy St. Jacques." He knew it was safe. He'd had a cover built under his own name; it was easier for many reasons. Who and what he really was was so buried, it would be nearly impossible to find.

Lettice flipped a perfectly manicured hand to the third person in their party. "And this is my granddaughter, Susan."

He smiled and nodded, just as he had at the boutique.

Susan smiled slightly in return, as if shy. She walked at a sedate pace, her movements rhythmic, languid. Sensual. His blood slowed and heated in response. The scent of perfume and the sea teased him. That he was hanging himself didn't seem to have an effect on his primitive side. One smile and he wanted her. He realized how careful he had been not to touch her when he'd relieved her loaded arms. Clearly some self-preservation was still functioning, but this was a complication he didn't need.

He focused his attention on the swathed-to-the-eyebrows grandmother between them.

"This is very kind of you," Lettice said, completely ignoring her earlier commandeering. "Are you here on vacation with your family?"

"Just myself. A little vacation and a little business." He grinned. It was the truth, after a fashion. "And you?"

"I live here for part of year. It's no big secret."

Lettice gestured toward the houses on the right side of the street.

He noticed both her arms were empty and smiled wryly. They reached her house, and he was careful to wait for Lettice to point it out before turning into the crushed-shell walkway. He set the basket and beach chair on the veranda, which stretched around the house. He would bet the wicker furniture set along it was imported from England.

Susan had been silent the entire time, but now as he faced her and handed back the lobster bag, she smiled and said, "I hope we haven't taken you out of your way, Mr. St. Jacques."

Her voice had an unexpectedly soft timbre, not at all the decisive tone of her grandmother's. It sent shivers racing down his spine, and he wanted to hear her speak again and again.

"You haven't," he said, realizing he was staring.

He couldn't stop, though. His gaze was trapped and held by her blue-green eyes. They were exactly the same color as her grandmother's, but they were far from shrewd and calculating. Lettice had displayed those qualities all too well. Susan's eyes were . . . he couldn't define the look they held as she stared back at him. He only knew he couldn't turn away.

"I'm glad we didn't inconvenience you," she finally said. "Even though my grandmother gave you no choice in the matter."

"She's charming," he murmured, desperately wanting to taste her perfectly curved lips.

The space between them seemed less, as something inside him pulled toward her. His breath was tight in his chest. He wanted to feel her mouth opening under his, her body twisting and turning in rising passion. . . .

"Well, thank you again, Mr. St. Jacques," Lettice said, effectively bringing them back to the real world.

Remy felt as if he were waking from an old witchwoman's voodoo spell. He looked away from Susan at the same time she looked away from him. She went inside the house before he could say a word.

He turned to the grandmother. Lettice was gazing at him with what could be only a look of speculation. Remy cleared his throat and said, "Glad to be of service. Good afternoon, ma'am."

He extricated himself from the veranda with a minimum of awkwardness. Back on the sidewalk, he lengthened his strides as much as possible without actually running away.

He'd been mesmerized by Susan. It was impossible that such a thing could have happened, and yet it had. The whole incident was disturbing. To be caught like that . . . and yet, she'd been so soft and feminine. He hadn't sensed a single calculation behind her actions. He knew his assignment had been compromised—and in the worst way— but he was floating. He couldn't help feeling he was back in the ninth grade at Loreauville High School and the most popular girl in the school had just smiled at him.

Maybe she had.

He had a name.

As she sat at a secluded table, Susan absently watched the people mingling about on the casino's upper floor. Half of Philadelphia had turned out for her grandmother's charity event, Côte d'Azur Night. Even some of Lettice's society friends were there—and everyone was dressed to the hilt, as was the custom in European casinos. Susan's mind, however, wasn't on the glitz and the glitter or the amount of proceeds Donald Trump would be turning over to Lettice. It was too busy replaying every aspect of the afternoon.

Remy St. Jacques was devastating close up. She had been helpless to do anything but stare at that lean, dark face that was all rough edges and virility. He possessed a smile of unexpected boyish charm, and it had nearly taken her breath. His voice was almost hoarse in timbre yet smooth, like expensive whiskey. And he had an accent, very slight and one she couldn't pinpoint. French, she thought, but not quite. She knew it would haunt her. She had a feeling everything about him would. It was embarrassing to know she'd been as dumbstruck as a Kevin Costner fan meeting her idol for the first time. What had happened to her usual cool? She'd met presidents and prime ministers with more poise than she'd exhibited that afternoon.

"He *was* intriguing."

Susan blinked at the sound of her grandmother's voice in her ear, then smiled as Lettice sat down at the table. She refused to pick up her grandmother's bait. Lettice had been teasing her since dinner about Remy St. Jacques. Good-natured teasing

"It's you, Grandmother," she said. "I keep telling you that."

Lettice grinned, a twinkle of satisfaction in her eye. "But he wasn't intrigued with me, dear."

Susan forced a casual laugh, knowing her grandmother *was* teasing. Lettice would be the last one to try to fix her up with some unknown. "Maybe it was the lobster."

Lettice chuckled. "Probably."

Sitting back, Lettice eyed Susan's gown. She'd done that several times, but had made no comment. Lettice had told her to wear "something glittery," but Susan supposed the high-necked, fitted beige silk by Bob Mackie might be too much for Philadelphia tastes. Under her Washington cover of flash, she'd worn clothes designed to be eye-catching. Tonight's gown was certainly that. The way the hand-beaded white and gold flowers flowed up and around her body and breasts was guaranteed to draw all eyes to her. It was funny to know that she would have worn it in a minute in Washington, but that night she was uncomfortable. That was partially why she had sought out a back table.

How far had she been seduced by the glamour and power, she wondered, until the sight of a briefcase full of money changed her world?

Deciding to halt the subject before it started, Susan said, "Everything looks wonderful tonight."

Lettice glanced around the room. "Mmm. I must say that even though I was dubious about this venture, the casino has done a splendid job. But you're sitting here by yourself, dear. Get out and mingle. Everyone is very interested in you, Susan."

She shrugged. "I just wanted a little quiet."

"There are several men, sons of some friends . . ." Lettice began.

"No, thank you, Grandmother," Susan said sternly. "I'll head off to the backwoods of Canada."

"Just a suggestion," Lettice said, rising from her chair. "I better get back to my own mingling— although those damn Longport people are all over me like bears on molasses."

Susan chuckled at her grandmother's description of the local society denizens. Most lived in Longport, the resort town at the far end of the barrier island. Lettice had a few choice words to say about the huge happy-face adorning Longport's water tower.

"And if I don't see you up and about, missy," Lettice continued, "I *will* drag out those men!"

"Five more minutes," Susan promised hastily.

It was four when her cousins found her. Ellen and Anne sat down, while Ellen's husband, Joe Carlini, and Anne's husband, James Farraday, rounded up a few more chairs.

"Hiding from Grandmother?" Ellen asked.

"Smart girl," Anne said.

Susan shook her head. It was hard to believe two very confident and elegant women could be so frightened of one spirited old lady.

"No, I'm not hiding, and you just missed her," she said.

"There are times when I'm glad Lettice is on my side," Joe said, sitting down next to his wife. He put his arm around Ellen and kissed her on the cheek. "Right, El?"

"Hardly," Ellen said. But she smiled at her husband.

"Are you sure she's not pushing you at some man?" Anne asked, leaning forward. There was a gleam in her eye that Susan swore could match any of Lettice's.

"I'm sure." Susan was laughing. She couldn't help it. One man came to mind, but she pushed the thought aside. "Anyway, do you see a man around?"

"No," James said. "But if there is, I almost feel sorry for the poor slob. . . ."

She was safely ensconced with people for the moment.

Remy knew the two men were with the other two women, but a shaft of jealousy ran through him at the thought that they were seeing that dress of hers up close. He desperately wanted to see it, too, but only him. Yet she had worn it for everyone else's eyes, not for his. She would never wear anything with just his pleasure in mind. The sooner he realized that, the sooner he'd get over these uncharacteristic physical responses to her. Deciding he could do just that with a drink, he strode inside the casino lounge.

Susan laughed as her cousin Anne said, "If there is a man around, then feel sorry for Susan."

James grinned. "You loved every minute of our courtship, Annie Farraday. Admit it."

"Never."

Susan smiled at her cousins. The individual coloring between the three of them was different, but they all shared the same blue-green eyes of their grandmother. Nearly all the younger Kitteridges were picking up Lettice's eye color, too. Funny, she mused, how a trait would run through a family despite the dilution of other genes.

"What's Washington like with the new administration?" Joe asked.

"It doesn't change," Susan said, then she laughed. "At least the parties don't."

"I never would have thought you'd be such a socialite," Anne said, her voice kind and uncritical. "I remember you were more serious as a kid."

Susan smiled. "I remember you always getting into trouble."

"She still does," James said, then dodged his wife's elbow to the ribs.

"We never got to see you much," Ellen said. "Not with Uncle Roddy being an ambassador."

"I was always sorry we didn't have an opportunity to be closer," Anne added.

Both cousins were concerned about her, Susan realized. It was obvious they were close and confided often in each other, something she'd never had the opportunity to do. She found the room suddenly intolerable, and had to force her smile and next words. "Grandmother said I could only have five minutes before I had to mingle with her guests, otherwise she would stick my head on a pike. I've been here ten, so if you don't mind . . ."

"Go," Ellen said. "You've taken your life in your hands as it is."

"And if Grandmother does have some man to introduce you to, run for the hills," Anne warned. "You could get stuck with someone like James!"

"Wait a minute!" James exclaimed as Ellen's husband laughed.

"Worse, you could get stuck with someone like Joe," Ellen said.

"What!"

Susan forced a last smile, then whirled away from the four of them. She had never envied Ellen and Anne before, but she did now. Both her cousins were adept businesswomen, Ellen joining in the Carlini Foods conglomerate and Anne running a prestigious stud farm. And it was so obvious that her cousins were in love and content. They had good men.

A strange emptiness filled her, digging deep down inside her. She couldn't even claim her profession, and she wasn't sure she wanted to. A deeper pain gnawed at her when she thought of her cousins' husbands. She hadn't been married to a good man, or even a mediocre one. She had been married to a traitor. There was no other word for Richard Ames, fast-rising State Department attaché who sold out for greed. No hidden ideology, no blackmail even, just money. And not that much of it. His selling secrets to the other side had come to light after he had been killed three years earlier in a car accident, and Susan still felt a rush of humiliation at being so fooled.

She had been just twenty-one when she met Richard, visiting her parents in England during summer vacation from college. Richard had been assigned to the embassy, and he had immediately begun to court her. Dazzled by him, she hadn't gone back to school. It had seemed so natural to marry him; it was a continuation of the life she knew and had thought she was expected to lead. All too soon after the wedding, she realized there was no true bond between her and Richard. Yes, the marriage had been a mistake from the beginning, but she had thought Richard was a good man—an honorable man—and so she had stayed with it. Very few people knew the truth about Richard. She owed Ross a great deal for that.

Another man came to mind. A man she didn't know, yet something inside her responded to him with a recognition that left her bewildered. She pushed the image away.

Realizing she was walking nowhere fast, Susan stopped by a bank of slot machines near the casino lounge. Soft dance music was coming from beyond the lounge doors.

Lord, she thought. She had to pull herself together. She had hidden herself away at the Jersey shore for a reason, and she needed to concentrate on that. Still, it hurt to know she couldn't go to anyone for advice. Ross Mitchelson had never been an easy man, but now he was downright puzzling. He was her boss at the Company, the term everyone used for the intelligence network at Langley, Virginia. He was also her friend. Ross had been investigating her husband's suspected sellout, and they had met after Richard's death. Ross had helped her through the revelation of Richard's selling State Department information, then had shrewdly suggested she could work for the Company as a courier, retrieving and passing on information. She had snapped the idea up, driven by the need to make amends for Richard. The Washington parties were perfect for it, and she, with her background, fit right in.

But Ross was taking bribes. That knowledge had shaken her faith in nearly everything. She had to stop the corruption, but she couldn't get past the way he had helped her after Richard had died. She just didn't know what to do, and so she did nothing. All of it was impossible for her conscience to cope with.

Lettice and her cousins were a temporary release for her. And Remy St. Jacques . . .

Susan realized he was standing only thirty feet away from her, on the threshold of the lounge. She had been staring at him and not seeing him. Or maybe she hadn't been seeing anything until he had come into sight.

He was wearing a summer suit and a black silk shirt. Not as formally dressed as some, but he wouldn't be out of place among the James Bond lookalikes. In fact, he was made for the part. His clothes were European, and there was no denying their expensive cut. He also wore a watchful cynicism she identified with 007. Move over Timothy Dalton, she thought in amusement.

He glanced at her, looked away, then back. His eyes widened as he took in her dress. Under his gaze the beige sheath didn't seem like much at all, she thought. She knew she should just smile, say hello, and walk away. But something overpowering demanded her schoolgirl performance of the afternoon be corrected.

She walked over to him. Being close to him felt a little like stepping in hot quicksand, but she gathered her control and held out her hand. "We met this afternoon. I'm Susan Kitteridge."

He took her hand in his. "I remember."

His touch combined with that distinctive voice were too much for her fragile hold on herself. The quicksand closed over her head. She tried to speak and couldn't.

"How was the lobster?" he asked.

"Delicious," she croaked out, then cleared her throat and said in near normal tones, "You were very nice this afternoon."

"No problem."

Something wiggled against her palm, and she realized he was trying to release her hand but she wasn't cooperating. Mortified, she yanked her hand back. This was definitely not one of her brightest moments.

"Are you enjoying Côte d'Azur Night?" she asked, and immediately wished she could call back the inane words.

"It's interesting," he said, smiling at her. "How about a drink? If you're not too busy, *chère*."

The endearment had been a natural and unexpected one, she realized as a shuttered look came over his face. The flicker of concern was gone, and he smiled as if he'd said nothing out of the ordinary. Susan raised her chin. If he could do it, then so could she.

"A drink would be nice."

He motioned toward the lounge and they walked in together. He didn't take her elbow to escort her or touch her in any way, and Susan found herself grateful and resentful at the same time.

The lounge was crowded and they leaned against the bar. They both ordered a club soda.

Remy chuckled. "We're certainly not going to make the bar rich tonight."

"True." He spoke English like a native, and yet there was that intriguing accent. "I've been trying to place your accent. Are you a transplanted Frenchman?"

"Close. French-Canadian."

"Ahh." She smiled, everything falling into place. "Quebec is a beautiful providence."

He shrugged.

The bartender arrived with their drinks, forestalling any further conversation. As Remy smiled and paid the young woman, Susan stared at his profile, drinking in the sharply defined features. His skin, dark and slightly reddened from the sun, was the shade of polished mahogany. She fought the urge to reach out and stroke his jawline.

The room was growing hotter and closer, and Susan struggled for control of herself as Remy finished paying the bartender. As a last-ditch effort she took a hefty swallow of her drink to cool off and tried conversation again. It beat the heck out of drooling.

"You said you were mixing business with vacation," she began.

"That's right. I'm in sales. I work for a company called CHT, and we produce chemicals and cleaners for various commercial uses. We're looking to open our northeastern U.S. market. I'm getting in a little vacation while I'm down here."

Susan nodded, deflated at the description. He was a salesman! That was so . . . ordinary. Not that there was anything wrong with ordinary, she quickly amended to herself. It was just that he looked so . . . un-ordinary.

She forced a smile. "That's fascinating."

"And that's very kind of you," he replied, grinning.

"No, no!" she said hastily, embarrassed that she'd been snobbish with him. "It *is* interesting. I mean, I'm sure there are a ton of nifty things that are needed every day that most people don't know about . . . I mean, chemicals are so complex . . . I mean, I'm dying here, Remy. Help me out of the hole I've dug for myself."

He laughed. "But you were going down faster than the *Titanic*, chère. Now, that was fascinating."

She made a face at him. "I bet.'"

"Then why don't we dance?"

She hesitated for a moment, wanting to and yet reluctant. Dancing with Remy St. Jacques could be dangerous. But the music was fast-paced, so she decided it was safe enough. "I'd love to."

As they walked toward the dance area, he took her hand, apparently so he wouldn't lose her in the crowd. Susan gritted her teeth as electric heat shot up her arm and down through her breasts and pelvis. It settled deep within her.

Matters were made worse when they reached the dance floor and the faster music seguèd into Lionel Richie's "Lady."

Remy gazed at her for a long moment, then

pulled her into his arms as if he'd been doing it for years. The shock of his body against hers ran through her, but her feet didn't stumble. To her relief, something inside her was working right, and she smoothly picked up the rhythm of his movements.

He held her right hand in close to their shoulders, his fingers enclosing hers in a gentle grip. Her breasts were pressing into his chest, and their lower torsos and thighs were brushing together with each step. Her temple was against his cheek, and she could feel his breath stirring her hair. Everything about him was lean, hard masculinity, and she was conscious of the way his one leg slipped naturally between her thighs for a second. It was just a touch of him against her in the most intimate of ways, then it was gone again. And it happened over and over. She wanted desperately to feel him fully and was shaking with fear that she'd lose all control right there, right then. The heat inside her was boiling, and the room was turning gray, fading. She took a deep breath in an effort to get air into her lungs, the fingers of her left hand digging into the material of his white jacket. Her feet, thank goodness, were still moving automatically.

His hand began to stroke her spine, and she stifled a moan of pleasure. He turned his head slightly and now her temple was no longer against his cheek. Instead, their lips were a bare inch apart. She was gasping for breath, and didn't care that he knew it.

She thought she heard him whisper her name, but she wasn't sure. The blood was roaring in her ears. Her body was making demands she was helpless to fight. She knew she should, but she couldn't remember why. She only knew that if she tilted her mouth slightly, they would . . .

The music abruptly switched to Bobby McFerrin's "Don't Worry, Be Happy." The noise level of the lounge immediately rose one hundred decibels. Remy straightened and set her away from him. Want and shock and relief washed through her simultaneously, leaving her drained.

Without a word he escorted her back to the bar. Susan let out her breath, wondering where all the air had come from. First she hadn't had any, now she had too much.

He literally dropped her off by her drink, saying, "I'm sorry, but I have to go now. It was nice seeing you again, Susan."

He walked out of the lounge before she could say a word. She stared at the spot where he'd been, then blinked, wondering if she'd dreamed the entire encounter.

If she had, she was in deeper trouble than she'd thought.

It was wrong. Everything was wrong.

Remy walked through the night, not caring where he was going.

He was furious with Susan for being so damn sensual and tempting. He was furious with himself for succumbing to her.

Maybe she had discovered who he truly was. Maybe someone had warned her that she was being watched.

He wished he could believe that but he knew better. He had wanted to meet her again. No matter how he wished he could deny it, he knew he'd be lying to himself. He had made only a half-hearted effort to hide himself in the casino. He should have reported in the first time she had seen him at that boutique. Now it was too late. He'd been badly compromised, as if he were a rookie police recruit and not a seasoned agent.

She had been too attractive from the beginning. He should have recognized how vulnerable he was. He knew what he should do now. He should call in and ask for a replacement. He should have done that after the boutique incident. To hell with his instincts, to hell with whatever wasn't quite right with the Susan Kitteridge assignment, and to hell with his pride, which had insisted he'd redeem himself with better care.

Remy cursed out loud. He had nearly lost all control on the dance floor with her. The scent of her, light and elusive, was still in his senses. Even now it was so easy to relive those moments, to feel her incredibly soft breasts against his chest, her thighs, warm and lush, against his legs. Dammit, clothes hadn't been a barrier. And that dress! The material had been so smooth under his palm, he'd caught himself caressing her back.

No more, he thought. He was getting nowhere fast by following her—except to be spotted, pressed into service, and nearly seduced. All of it was his own doing.

He stopped and looked around, realizing he had no idea where he was. On some dark street in Atlantic City. Or maybe New York. He had been walking for hours.

Well, it was time to admit the truth. He had to call Ross and report his star veteran was a dismal failure.

He turned around and starting walking back the way he had come. First, he had to find a phone.

• • •

He watched her and her grandmother walk up the steps and onto the boardwalk.

The brilliant sun beat down on him. He had found a telephone the night before, but he hadn't used it. Instead, another idea had come to him. A very daring idea. One he knew Ross wouldn't approve of. Ross would scream his head off . . . if he knew.

Remy smiled. His own instincts approved of what he was doing. In fact, they had gone off like light bulbs at a General Electric demonstration.

He waited until they were well onto the boardwalk, then deliberately walked over to them.

"Good day, ladies."

Three

Remy took the beach chair and basket from Susan before she could stop him. "It's a pleasure to see you ladies again. Allow me to help you, Susan."

If he couldn't discover what her habits were from the outside, he told himself, he certainly could from the inside. It was risky, but at the rate he was going, being on the inside was much less risky than being spotted every two minutes.

"How very nice," Lettice said, smiling at him. She was lost in a bold yellow and green caftan and sun hat.

Susan, however, was very . . . unlost in a one-piece turquoise bathing suit and wraparound skirt. He could see enough of her upper body to know the suit had side cutouts. His heart pounded hard in anticipation of seeing her satiny flesh.

"I really enjoyed Côte d'Azure Night," he said as they strolled along the boards. "But I must apologize for running out on you like that, Susan. I've been negotiating a deal in Vancouver, and I was to call them after midnight our time. I hope you can forgive me."

"You ran out on her?" Lettice asked, looking from him to Susan. "You didn't tell me Mr. St. Jacques was at the casino last night, Susan."

"Remy," Remy said.

"Remy."

Susan shrugged. "We just had a drink together in the lounge." She shrugged again. "There's no need to apologize . . . Remy."

He smiled. "I feel there is, and I do."

She had left it with her grandmother at only a drink, he mused. Had she been affected by their dancing as he? Had she felt how their bodies fit perfectly, as if made for each other? The heat created by their hips and thighs brushing together with every step? Had she been as mindless and out of control as he?

The notion was gratifying . . . and dangerous.

They arrived at the row of cabanas along the back of the beach, and he helped the women unload their things at theirs. Neither Lettice nor Susan asked him to join them, but neither looked distressed when he set up a few feet away. He hadn't expected an invitation, but he was pleased that they didn't seem to mind him. The last thing he needed was to irritate either of them into avoiding him.

He had brought only a towel and some sunscreen, so it took him just a moment to set up for a day of sunbathing. He settled onto the towel and leaned back on his elbows, breathing in the sea air, its tangy, salty aroma overlaid with the odor of coconut-scented tanning lotion. An old biplane was flying across the hazy blue sky, trailing a message that read GET STUFFED AT THE LOBSTER HOUSE. 44TH AND THE BOARDWALK.

Half-naked bodies lay everywhere in an adolescent boy's dream. But Remy was an adult, and none drew his gaze like the slender, dark-haired woman standing in front of the Kitteridge cabana.

She untied her skirt and slowly unwrapped it from her hips, revealing large diamond-shaped cutouts in her suit. His hands ached to caress the skin she'd exposed to his gaze. Her thighs were as lush as he remembered. A big gold bracelet dangled from one wrist.

His blood roared in his ears, and he took a deep breath to control his reaction. It didn't help. She was a witchwoman, his witchwoman.

He peeled off his black t-shirt, then snatched up the sunscreen and stood. He was clad only in a pair of white jams and canvas scuffs, downright prudish when compared to the bikinis some men were wearing. Taking a deep breath, he walked over to the cabana.

"I wonder if I could beg a favor, ladies."

Susan was in the process of spreading a cotton blanket on the sand. She looked up, her eyes wide with some hidden emotion. The upper swells of her breasts were just visible above the heart-shaped bodice of the bathing suit.

He wanted to stroke them, run his palms over the silken mounds, and undo the suit straps. His fingers tightened around the small bottle in his hand.

With a gargantuan effort he forced himself to turn away from the beautiful sight before him and hold out the bottle to the grandmother. "Ma'am, I wouldn't be asking if I had arms long enough to reach all of my back."

Lettice stared at him, her eyes narrowing. "I'm not a fool, young man."

"I expect not," he said, smiling angelically. "You

remind me of my own grandmama, Mrs. Kitteridge. She has a tart tongue too."

"You almost went too far on that one," Lettice said, taking the sunscreen from him. "Turn around and squat down. I'm not some six-foot blonde, you know."

"You're much more beautiful."

"Oh, brother," Susan murmured from behind him.

Lettice smacked him on the arm. "Just turn around."

Remy grinned and turned around. Obeying Lettice's command, he bent slightly so she could reach his back. Susan was lying on her stomach, her face buried in her folded arms, her shoulders shaking suspiciously. She was laughing . . . and providing him with a view of a long, lovely back and curving hips.

"You mentioned you were here on business," Lettice said, rubbing in the lotion with such vigor, the primitive urges inside him were thoroughly squelched.

He cleared his throat. "Yes, ma'am. I'm with CHT, in Canada."

"You're Canadian?"

"French-Canadian." His Acadian ancestors had stood him in good stead many times—and the foreign nationality made his cover much more complicated to dig through. "My company makes chemicals and cleaners for commercial uses, and we've been wanting to open up the markets in the northeastern United States. I was on a three-week tour of the major cities, Bangor, Boston, down to Baltimore. Atlantic City is my last stop."

Susan raised her head. "What kind of commercial uses?"

Her eyes were wide and unblinking as she looked at him.

He gazed steadily back, then said in a low voice, "Water softeners, septic cleaners for water treatment, cleaners for hospitals and restaurants. That type of thing."

"Well, that's a non-gigolo occupation if I ever heard one," Lettice said.

"Grandmother!"

"I've heard better, believe me!"

Remy laughed. The last thing he had expected to be mistaken for was a gigolo. His amusement faded when he thought of what he really was.

"I admit I do have an unglamorous job," he said. It was the truth. "But . . . well, you've both been very nice, but if you are worried that I'm . . . latching on to you, I can leave."

Lettice slapped him on the back. "I was only teasing. Besides, I picked you up, remember? You're done."

He stood. "Maybe I should fear for my virtue."

Susan collapsed in laughter.

"And what's the matter with you, missy?" Lettice snapped, glaring at her granddaughter.

"I think he's right," Susan gasped between fits of giggles.

Remy chuckled as Lettice stammered indignantly.

"I should be so lucky," he said.

Lettice nodded. "Damn straight."

He walked over to his towel and settled on his stomach.

Susan, too, was baking her back. She smiled at him, knowledge and amusement apparent in her expression. He smiled back.

He was in.

•   •   •

"You don't suppose he really is after me?"

Susan choked at her grandmother's speculative tone. She stopped the porch swing and studied her grandmother, but couldn't tell if Lettice was being serious or not.

"Weeeell . . ." Susan drew out the word. "It's possible. Although he'd have to be pretty desperate—"

"In a pig's eye!" Lettice ruffled up like an outraged hen.

Susan chuckled and shook her head. "Really, Grandmother. You've been throwing yourself at the poor man. Or lobsters."

"I do not throw myself at men, Susan," Lettice snapped, rustling the afternoon newspaper she was reading. She tossed a section to the foot of her lounge chair. "I have been known to attract men upon occasion. And they were not desperate!"

"I'm sure," Susan murmured, and pushed the swing into motion again.

She stared out at the orange sun of late afternoon and smiled to herself. Remy had spent the day with them on the beach. He'd flirted with Lettice, who enjoyed it thoroughly. And, Susan thought, didn't take it seriously. At least her grandmother hadn't seemed to until her question.

Lettice was kidding again. She was an expert in the field of bait and tease.

Susan resisted a sigh, remembering when Remy had taken off his T-shirt. He had a long well-proportioned torso, and his skin had been biscuit-colored with the faint glow of last year's tan. His muscles were defined but not bulky, just lean and fit. And his upper chest and stomach had been covered in a fine mat of dark hair.

She had tried so hard not to stare at him as he

lay a few feet away from her, but she had. She must have. She couldn't remember looking away from him even once. Her hands had shook with the effort to keep from touching him. The sun had baked her outside, and a need she'd been barely able to control had radiated her on the inside. She had wanted him, wanted to feel his mouth on hers, his body tight against her own. If Lettice hadn't been here, she would have reached out for him. Heat still scalded her face at the thought.

And yet she had enjoyed herself thoroughly. She hadn't expected to, especially since she'd been still wary with him over the night before, apology or no. Although completely aware of him at a primitive level the entire time they were on the beach, she had also been relaxed and content just to lie there and talk. Her caution had faded, and she had enjoyed the company.

"I like him," Lettice said.

Susan glanced over and smiled. "So do I."

Lettice set down the paper and gazed at her granddaughter. "There's something not right with him, you know."

The swing stopped. "What do you mean?"

Lettice frowned. "I don't know. I can't put my finger on it. That was why I threw out that comment about him not being like a gigolo."

"But you picked him up—" Susan stopped. "We had both seen him before that."

"True. I've also seen a dozen people over and over since we've been here. Atlantic City is not a big town, and people do rub elbows, so to speak. That's not unusual." Lettice shrugged. "We spend our lives making sure our friends and our lovers are that because of us, not what the name Kitteridge brings. But I can't help being suspicious, especially when I sense there's more to him than just a salesman. As if he's hiding something. Time will tell if he is. In the meantime, you be careful, Susan."

"I'm not a fool, Grandmother."

Lettice smiled with satisfaction. "Neither am I, Susan. Although I suspect you'll tell me what *you're* hiding when you're ready."

Susan refused to allow the tiniest muscle in her face to move. "I'm not hiding anything, Grandmother."

"You've been walking around like a zombie since you got here. Is it a man?"

"No."

Lettice raised an eyebrow, and Susan knew she had been too forceful with her answer. "Well, see that Remy St. Jacques isn't another mistake."

Susan hesitated for a long moment, then nodded. Her grandmother had a point.

Later, after dinner, Susan sat in a wing chair in the library. Lettice was busy in the kitchen with her housekeeper, Mamie, so Susan didn't make a pretense of reading the book she held in her hand.

She was succumbing to Remy St. Jacques, and she knew it.

Usually she was cautious, but not a single alarm bell had gone off in her head about him. That was very dangerous. Lettice was right; she should be careful. The situation with Ross left her vulnerable in other areas. But she wasn't ready to condemn Remy as a fortune hunter. There might be something "not right" about him, but there was also something "not wrong."

She gazed at the telephone atop a bamboo and glass table. Her grandmother had called her a zombie, and she had to admit Lettice wasn't far from the truth. It was getting easier to set Ross's accepting a bribe further and further from her mind. If only she could.

She had walked away from Washington without a word to him. Now she wondered if she had not been trying to walk away from the problem. Maybe that was a mistake. Maybe she should have confronted Ross about the money. Maybe he had an explanation for it, one she hadn't considered.

She only had to call a number, and it would be all over. She could discuss it with Ross, perhaps persuade him to do the right thing. He might already be doing the right thing. She could at least stop the war going on inside her.

She could also ask for a check on Remy, just to see that he really was a salesman for a chemical company.

She set down her unread book and stood up. She walked over to the telephone. She picked up the receiver.

Something rose inside her in violent protest, and she set the receiver back down again. Relief washed through her.

She picked the receiver up again . . . and froze again.

Clearly some part of her brain didn't like the idea of a telephone call.

She set the receiver in its cradle once more and walked away.

"You're not doing anything except going to the beach?"

Hearing the disbelief in Ross's voice, Remy tightened his fingers around the pay phone's receiver. "And dinner. And the casinos. Typical things."

"Mmm. She's extremely clever, Remy. And very ruthless."

Remy was surprised at Ross's straightforward comments. Usually they talked around things for security's sake.

"Is something wrong?" he asked, his whole body tensing.

"No. No. Just don't take any chances."

It was a little too late for that, Remy thought wryly. Still, ruthless didn't jibe with the memory of Susan in the lingerie boutique, staring off into space. It had been a moment when she didn't have to act for her grandmother, when she was alone, or thought she was. Even the greatest actors drop their roles when they're sure they're offstage. He knew Susan, as a low-grade courier, didn't have the training for deception that some received. He couldn't imagine her being this good on just talent alone. And there were other things about her, little things that denied a calculating nature.

He was about to open his mouth and say something to Ross, but the man continued.

"Do you think she's leading you around by the nose?"

"Lower," he muttered in a bare breath.

"What?"

"I was just clearing my throat."

This was the time to tell his boss about connecting with Susan and now being on the inside. Ross wouldn't like it, he was sure. In fact, Ross would probably call him off and put someone else on. Someone who went too much by the book. Someone who might not pick up the conflicting signals about Susan. Someone who might just handle it very quickly . . . and very thoroughly.

"The situation is under control," he told Ross.

"Well, fine then. Be sure and give my love to Louise."

Remy grinned. Louise was Ross's cat. "I will."

"I appreciate what you're doing for me."

"No problem." He realized he meant it on some level.

The connection ended. Remy slowly hung up the phone. He had committed the sin of omission with Ross, something he had never done before.

He actually felt good about it.

And that worried him.

"Will you have dinner with me tonight?"

Remy watched as Susan's eyes widened in surprise at the request. Lettice had already gone into the house, after having said something about playing keno with the neighbors. He had immediately taken advantage of his moment alone with Susan. What, he wondered in amusement, had she thought her "businessman" was hanging around for? Her grandmother?

"Well, I . . ."

"I'd really appreciate it, *chère*," he said, "if you would take pity on a poor lonely soul."

She laughed. "You are *not* a poor soul, Remy."

He smiled, liking the way she laughed. "Well, it was worth a try."

He had joined the two women again at the beach, just as he had the day before. This time they seemed to have half expected him. At least nobody looked very surprised, and he again had the pleasure and torture of watching Susan.

Ross's warning had swirled through his head, and he had carefully watched her every movement for signs that might give her away. She carried the women's things with an occasional glance of affectionate exasperation at her grandmother. Her hand went out in an automatic and solicitous gesture to help Lettice down the wooden steps from the boardwalk. She seemed to enjoy their leisurely pace, as if she had all the time in the world. And she didn't look around at the sunbathers, suggesting that she was watching for someone. One would think that with the passing of time, she would be growing anxious about handing over whatever it was she had rather than being more relaxed.

Just little things.

They were enough to make him want to start putting his instincts to the test.

"So, Susan Kitteridge," he asked in a formal voice, "will you have dinner with me?"

She looked around, then to his complete surprise leaned forward in a conspirator's stance. He wondered what she had in mind. Perfume swirled through his senses. She was so close that his heart, in a Pavlovian response, began to pound.

"I'm dying for a pizza on the boardwalk."

He blinked, then chuckled. "You got it. I'll pick you up at eight?"

She smiled, and his heart flipped. "Fine."

Later that night they sat in a little open air pizza shop and wolfed down slices of thin-crusted spicy pizza. Susan was grinning as she wiped sauce from the side of her mouth with a paper napkin. Remy wished he were the lucky napkin. He'd love to be next to those incredible lips. To be honest, he'd wished for a lot of things since he picked Susan up and seen her in her red cotton gauze vest and skirt. Delicate sandals added to the "cool breeze" effect.

Even now under the harsh lights, her skin glowed and the brilliant red of her outfit emphasized the rich darkness of her hair. Her blue-green eyes were more vivid than ever before. The vest clung to her breasts and outlined her slender waist. He had only to undo the little gold buttons to expose her flesh to his hands . . . his mouth.

She made him forget so many things.

He had noticed she was more friendly and relaxed with him now than the other night in the casino. He didn't know if it was the casual atmosphere or being away from her grandmother. It was clear she was enjoying herself. So was he.

He looked around at the occupied tables. The pizzeria had been hot when they'd first come in. Suddenly it seemed hotter with all the humanity shoehorned into the little dining room. "This place is getting crowded," he said. "Why don't we take our last slices and walk along the boardwalk, where it's cooler?"

"Good idea." She rose picking up her pizza and drink. Then frowned at her purse, still lying on the table.

"No way!" Remy said, standing and holding his own meal.

She chuckled and set down her drink, slung the bag's strap up on her shoulder, then picked up her drink again.

The temperature plunged twenty degrees the moment they stepped out of the tiny shop.

Remy sighed as they walked along the boards. "Much better."

"Would you have carried my purse to get out here?" she asked, grinning at him.

"It's a moot point."

"You don't strike me as a man who would be reluctant to carry a purse."

"No man is 'reluctant,' *chère*," he replied after taking a sip of his drink. "It's just that you women have brainwashed us into thinking it's unmasculine. Men carried purses for centuries until women demanded the right to do so."

"I will be happy to help you break the mold by allowing you to carry mine."

"I appreciate the offer, believe me, but I for one don't want the damn thing falling off my shoulder every two minutes."

"Party-pooper."

He finished off the last of his pizza and drink, shoved the napkin and cup into the nearest receptacle, then waved his now-free hands.

"Personally," he said, "I think men have finally gotten the better of the bargain."

"That's just an excuse."

Her purse strap dropped with a thump to the crook of her elbow. They both laughed.

"I may not want to carry it, but I can help," Remy said, lifting the strap back up to her shoulder. Then he switched around to her other side. "Here. I'll hold it while you eat."

He encircled her shoulders with his arm, his fingers casually entwining the purse strap.

"That was smooth," Susan said dryly.

"I thought so."

He liked the feel of her walking next to him. She was taller than average, and their strides were comfortable together. The side of her breast was only inches from his chest, and the feel of her soft, warm flesh beneath his hand was intoxicating. Her hip brushed his every so often.

"Eat your pizza, *chère*, and I'll take you for a walk on the moonlit beach."

"Sorry." She swallowed a bite and pointed toward

the dark sand to their right. A patrol jeep was stopped next to a group of teenagers. A short conversation ensued, and the kids turned around and began walking back toward the boardwalk.

"Ah, well," Remy said. "The best laid plans . . ."

"Ahem. Very bad pun."

"Sorry."

He made sure he kept the evening light, with a little browsing and a lot of walking. The attraction he felt battled with his common sense and caution as his awareness of her grew. He also realized how much she had deferred to her grandmother before, staying out of the conversational spotlight. Now she let her quick wit shine. He doubted she was emerging from a cocoon like a shy butterfly. It merely indicated her ability to adapt to the situation, and that was to be expected. She wouldn't have been picked for her job if she wasn't able to blend in.

By the time they returned to her grandmother's home, Ross's warning was fading from Remy's mind. He thought he had proven a point, but the problem was he couldn't remember what it was supposed to be.

"I enjoyed the walk and the pizza," Susan said, smiling at him. She pushed her house key into the lock and turned it.

"So did I."

He reached out and covered her fingers with his. She stilled and looked up at him. As he stared into her incredible eyes, their expression expectant and reluctant at the same time, Ross's warning went clear out of his head.

He leaned forward and touched his lips to hers.

Slowly she responded with a gentle kiss. He lifted her hand away from the doorknob and put it on his shoulder as he pulled her closer. Her body melted against his, until her breasts pressed to his chest, her thighs just touching his. Her mouth was drugging, moist and sweet and heated. Light, airy perfume teased his senses as always. He didn't want to hurry anything. He wanted to taste her all night.

But a taste was too much and not nearly enough. He crowded her against him, even as her arms wound tightly around his neck. Their tongues surged together in rising need. His blood roared through him, like a train out of control. Something else was in control, driving him to the brink of exquisite extinction. . . .

Susan suddenly broke away. She was out of his arms before he could stop her.

"Good night, Remy."

He straightened and cleared his throat. "Good . . ."

She opened the front door, stepped inside, and shut it.

". . . night."

He stared at the stained glass inserts.

He was in trouble. Deep trouble.

Four

"Are you crazy!"

Susan smiled at her grandmother, refusing to respond in like anger. Lettice was angry enough for the two of them.

"No, I am not crazy," she said, even though she had thought just that throughout her sleepless night. Something inside her automatically rebelled at hearing her own doubts said out loud. "It was just a casual date."

Lettice glared at her across the breakfast dishes. "The way he kissed you was hardly casual, missy!"

Susan's jaw dropped in astonishment. "You saw?"

Lettice smiled sweetly. "The entire world saw, dear. You were under the porch light. And I was leaving Joan's at the time."

Susan could feel her face heating at the idea of being seen by the neighbors . . . and the town . . . and the state . . . and Rona Barrett. Geraldo would probably do an exposé. . . .

"Grandmother, calm down!" she exclaimed, her panic momentarily rising to a crescendo pitch.

"I will not calm down," Lettice said in more matter-of-fact tones. "Not when you go around kissing a man you don't even know like that."

Susan forced herself under control. It was just one kiss, for goodness' sake. She tried a little joke. "Are you sure you're not jealous?"

"Jealous!" Lettice slapped her knife down on the bamboo and glass table. "You are not too old for me to wash your mouth out with soap!"

Susan looked heavenward, not believing the entire conversation. She was twenty-nine years old and way past lectures on behavior from her grandmother. Still, there was something about the way Lettice looked, disapproving and disappointed at the same time, that made her feel slightly ashamed. Ellen and Anne were exposed to it all the time. No wonder they lived in fear of Lettice.

"Grandmother, please," she said, pushing away her cup of tea. "I'm sorry. It was only a joke, a poor one."

"Very poor." Lettice snorted in disgust. "I can see that you're losing your common sense with Mr. St. Jacques. I'm going to have to do something about that."

Fear shot through Susan. She had a feeling that it was time to pack for the Canadian backwoods. "Look, Grandmother, there's no need to get . . . that upset. I'm not making a big deal out of kissing Remy, so you shouldn't. Besides, we have no evidence that he is a fortune hunter, and only two days ago you didn't think he was. One kiss shouldn't change that—"

"It might."

The way Remy had pulled her against him, the

way his mouth had fitted to hers, the way the passion had risen in her, swift and unrelenting, flashed through Susan. She set her jaw to dispel the feeling that still haunted her.

Somehow, she had managed to break away from Remy's devastating kiss and escape into the house. Didn't her grandmother know the effort that had taken? And if Lettice didn't, then Susan was damn well not going to tell the woman.

Lettice stared at her for a moment, then sighed. "It's just that I worry about you. You haven't been the same since Richard died, Susan. You've been gallivanting all over Washington. . . . The stories have come home, child."

Susan refused to open her mouth and say anything. Her stomach turned over, and the hairs on her arms rose from a sudden chill. She hated this, but what could she say? *Don't worry, Grandmother, it's all a cover because I'm a spy?* Hardly.

"I'm okay, Grandmother. Believe me. And you are fussing too much over a date for pizza and a walk on the boards." She refused to admit she was trying to convince herself as much as her grandmother, but she was tired of living with suspicion and distrust. Remy's actions would speak for him.

Anyway, she had something else to deal with . . . and she'd better start dealing with Ross soon. This limbo was almost too appealing.

"I'm not so sure that kiss was casual," Lettice said again, but she was looking more relaxed. Not much more, Susan admitted, but maybe enough to let her granddaughter squeak through with a little push.

"I have your genes, Lettice Kitteridge," she said,

grinning. "I am not going to fall for Remy St. Jacques over one kiss."

Lettice eyed her for a long moment, then nodded. "Good."

Susan nodded back, remembering the way his mouth felt, soft and demanding, spinning her into a sensual oblivion. Any woman would have fallen for a man who could kiss like that, yet she hadn't.

She was terrified she'd already done it with just one look.

Remy came later to the beach that day. He immediately noticed a difference in Lettice. She was still friendly, but he sensed she was measuring him.

He forgot the notion the moment Susan smiled at him.

Her curving lips held a shared intimacy that left him gasping for air. Lord, but he wanted to taste them again, feel them part in the passion he'd created inside her. A man could live on Susan's kisses. He had no idea what would have happened if she hadn't pulled away when she did. He probably would have disgraced himself and been damned glad of it too.

It took every effort to spread out his towel and settle on the sand near her. Not next to her. Not close. He didn't trust himself for that.

"How long will you be here?" Lettice asked from inside her cabana.

He gazed at Susan. He could almost feel her breasts pressed against his chest again, her flesh like satin under his hands. He shrugged casually. "It all depends. How long will you be here?"

"Not that long."

"Grandmother, look at that baby in the pink bikini over there," Susan interrupted, pointing toward a young family settling in several feet away. The beach was crowded and a few inches of sand was serving as a privacy barrier between people.

"My goodness, what a little sweetie!" Lettice exclaimed, smiling in pleasure.

Remy frowned at Lettice, now that her attention was diverted. Maybe she didn't like Susan going out with him. He supposed it could just be caution on her part. After all, her granddaughter was the equivalent of a Garden District heiress back home—beautiful and socially elite. He'd run into one or two of them way back, when he'd been a detective on the New Orleans police force. Still, the word *gigolo* came to him, and he hid a smile of amusement. If she only knew the truth . . .

Guilt surfaced instantly. What he was doing was far worse, and he knew it.

As Lettice fussed and cooed over the baby, Susan turned to Remy and smiled at him. He was mesmerized by the look of intimacy she gave him. Had any other man received that look from her, he wondered, and a hot bolt of jealousy ripped through him.

"How old is she?" Lettice called out to the proud mother.

"Eight months, ma'am."

"She's beautiful." Lettice smiled at the baby, who actually smiled back.

The woman turned to her husband, who was struggling to put up a beach umbrella, and told him to be sure to set up the portable crib in the shade. Remy froze. He knew perfectly well what the woman had said; the problem was she had said it in French. A French he had heard all too often the last several days from the hundreds of French-Canadians who had come to the New Jersey shore. It was a French as different from his own as a Bronx gang member's English was from an Oxford scholar's. He had been grateful for being able to blend in so well . . . until now. He hoped the couple stayed to themselves.

"I beg your pardon . . ." Lettice called out to the woman.

Remy could feel his muscles tense.

". . . but you speak so beautifully. Are you from Canada or France?"

"Quebec," the woman said.

Lettice smiled triumphantly. "Our friend, Mr. St. Jacques, is from Canada also."

Immediately the woman greeted him in their "native" tongue. Remy cursed silently. If he answered her in French, chances were she'd recognize his dialect wasn't hers and ask about it. He didn't know how well-versed in the language either Lettice or Susan were. But worse, if he didn't answer in French, the couple would think him rude . . . and so would Susan and her grandmother.

Either way he'd be starting the seeds of suspicion for Susan to pick up and follow.

"Is that one of your towels over there?" he asked, pointing to a towel lying crumpled and unclaimed on the sand behind the family.

The woman turned, *"Oui."*

Remy leapt into action. "I'll get it."

He scrambled over to the towel and snatched it up before anyone else could move.

"There you go," he said, handing it back to the woman. Then he asked boldly, "Where in Quebec?"

"Quebec, the city," the man answered.

"I'm from Montreal." Remy shrugged at the lack of further common ground between them. "The waters are definitely warmer here, I find."

"Definitely."

He kept to English and directed a look to Lettice and Susan, trying to signal to the man that it would be impolite to speak a language they couldn't understand.

The man glanced at the two women and smiled, clearly understanding the message.

"So many of us come down here now," the man said in English. "It should be called the Canadian Riviera."

Remy relaxed and chuckled. "I think it is."

The rest was easy, and when Remy returned to his towel he counted himself lucky to have squeaked through the moment with his "countrymen."

Still, Lettice was definitely suspicious. He couldn't help that. He was not about to give up the ground he'd already claimed with Susan.

His own suspicion about Susan had already become belief. If she were a traitor, he'd eat his damn baseball cap. Something was going on, though. Something that involved her, whether she was aware of it or not. He was determined to find out just what that something was. In the meantime he had to protect her as best he could.

His gaze drifted to her breasts, barely contained in a bandeau top.

It would be a pleasure.

"You really don't have to carry our things back. Susan and I are perfectly capable, you know."

"But it's a pleasure, Mrs. Kitteridge. Besides, you have been so kind to me, allowing a lonely man to join you every day."

"I suppose."

Susan smothered a chuckle at her grandmother's aggrieved tone. Lettice had been hoisted by her own petard, as the saying went. She had a feeling her grandmother didn't know how to "unlike" Remy, but she was trying her best. Susan was sure Lettice had had a point with the couple at the beach. No one but her would ever know what it was now, thanks to a towel.

She smothered another giggle.

As she looked at Remy's profile, though, she knew Lettice was right. There was more to him than a salesman. He possessed a subtle underlying current of power. How odd. There was nothing odd about his hard, lean body, about the way his hands heated her flesh wherever he touched her. Or the way his nearness drove her into a state of helpless awareness.

One phone call, she thought as they walked silently along. All she had to do was pick up the telephone and ask to have him checked. Then she would know Remy St. Jacques.

A solid wall of resistance welled up inside her. She supposed Lettice was right, but she hated the thought of not giving the man a chance to prove himself on his own terms. It was dishonest as much as it was cautious. She had had enough of dishonesty to last a lifetime. All she needed to do was exercise a little personal caution and let events unfold at their own pace.

Dammit, she thought, what events? He hadn't said a word to her about last night. He hadn't asked her out again. She thought he'd given her several intimate signals. At least there had been moments when he'd looked at her with lambent, hungry eyes. Maybe it had been indigestion.

They reached the house, and Susan glanced up, surprised. She hadn't realized exactly where they were at first. As Remy set the beach chairs and basket on the veranda, regret combined with anger swelled inside her. Would he leave without a word?

"Good-bye, Mrs. Kitteridge," he said to her grandmother.

Lettice nodded almost curtly, clearly grumpy at being thwarted earlier. "Good-bye."

He turned to Susan, and she didn't move as he stared at her for a long moment. She was trapped by his indefinable expression.

"Come walk with me for a few minutes."

It was a demand—soft and gentle, but a demand nonetheless.

"She has to get ready for supper, Remy," Lettice broke in. "And we're going to see my sister tomorrow. We have to get ready for that too."

Susan gritted her teeth at her grandmother's quick answer. She wasn't a kid, for goodness' sake!

"I'll be glad to take a walk."

"Susan," Lettice said in warning tones.

"Down by the bay?" she asked, ignoring her grandmother. The house was about equal distance from the ocean and the bay.

"Perfect."

"Susan."

Her grandmother's lips were pursed in disapproval, and Susan could imagine that forbidding look had sent people scurrying before. She smiled and patted her grandmother's cheek.

"I *do* need to talk to Remy, Grandmother. Remember?"

Lettice blinked.

"I'll be fine. Don't worry about this stuff. I'll take care of it when we get back." She turned back to Remy. "Shall we go?"

They stepped off the porch together. He didn't touch her, but his body was so close, she could feel her nerve endings sizzle with awareness. When they were out of sight of the house, he finally spoke.

"This is not inconvenient?"

She ducked her head, suddenly feeling shy. "No. It's fine."

They walked along. He didn't take her hand. She didn't offer it. Maybe he was going to tell her last night's kiss was a mistake, she thought. Maybe she ought to be grateful if he did.

The bay was quiet. It had no pounding surf; the waters, instead, lapped gently on the sand. This side of the island was given over to the horseshoe crabs and the dunes.

By mutual consent they picked a small bluff overlooking the beach and sat down among the seagrasses. Susan fiddled nervously with the knotted tails of her shirt. Remy kept his gaze directed toward the bay. The afternoon sun was a dull yellow and low in the sky.

The space between them was like a chasm.

"Finally," he said. "Away from the Dragon Queen."

Susan giggled, realizing his problem had not been the kiss, but Lettice. The odd tension left her. "I understand she has that effect. But I love her dearly."

He looked at her. "I like her too. But she doesn't make it easy, *chère*."

She smiled in answer.

Their amusement slowly gave way to something more. Remy's gaze grew hot, and he set his jaw as if he were losing his control. She couldn't look away from him, the warmth inside her changing to want. Heat rippled along her senses. The need coursing through her was overwhelming.

He reached out and touched her hair, just the ends. She closed her eyes, took a deep breath, and opened them again.

"You were unexpected, Susan Kitteridge," he said in a bare whisper. "Did you know that?"

"Yes."

"You confuse me, *chère.*"

Desire raged through her. If he touched her further . . . Lord help her, but she wanted him to, needed him to. She lifted weightless fingers and traced the hard line of his jaw. A shudder ran through him.

"Remy, please."

Their mouths met in soft fire. The pleasure rocked her, and she fitted her lips to his eagerly, her tongue swirling with his. His hands were firm on her shoulders, holding her in place. All the doubts and fears disappeared in the dark sensuality he evoked.

Her arms went around his neck, pulling him tightly to her, and they tumbled down onto the warm sand of the dunes. His body covered hers heavily, pressing the air out of her lungs. She wanted it, needed it.

The kiss was hot and drugging, driving her into a sweet insanity. She ran her hands down his back until she found the bottom of his tank top. She pushed it up as her fingers swept across his heated skin. His muscles were like hard iron and they flexed under her touch, sending her senses spinning toward oblivion.

His hands skimmed across her body. She moaned

when his fingers slipped beneath her shirt and traced the top edge of her suit. They edged inside. She moaned again when his thumb rubbed across her nipple. She had never felt this intense reaction to a man before. He wasn't artful in seduction, and she wasn't being seduced. She had known from the beginning their attraction to each other was strong, almost overwhelming. There was a clean honesty between them, something she didn't think she'd ever experienced with a man.

He cupped her breast and buried his lips in the soft column of her throat. She gasped, her blood coursing wildly through her veins. She didn't care about anything—where they were, who they were. She just wanted this to go on forever.

But it couldn't.

Slowly, reality set in, and she was aware of open sky and calling sea gulls . . . and voices on the beach below.

"Remy." She ran her hands up and down his back, almost drawing out his heat. "People."

He trailed kisses along her cheek. "Tell them we got here first, *chère.*"

She chuckled, her pulse slowing to a more normal rate. Patting his back, she dropped his shirt into place. "I don't think it will work."

"Damn." But he stopped, only his rapid breathing a sign of the passion he'd experienced.

They lay until the voices drifted farther away, then sat up together. Susan grinned sheepishly as he brushed the sand from her back. It was almost as if a faucet had been abruptly shut off in both of them. She knew it wouldn't take much to open it again, though.

"I believe you wanted to talk to me," she said innocently.

"I think I just did."

They rose to their feet, reluctant to leave. Now that the beachcombers were far down the shoreline, Susan knew it would be easy to succumb to desire again. But common sense and the thought of Lettice finally won out.

Remy held her hand on the way back. She realized she was being foolish about him, but she couldn't seem to help herself. Ross Mitchelson had been a heavy weight on her conscience for weeks, yet she was finding it easier and easier to shrug him away. She had been seduced by distraction. Remy was very good at distracting.

"Will you go to dinner with me tonight?" he asked.

She sighed. Her hand felt warm and unexpectedly safe in his. "I'd love to, but I ought to keep the peace."

"She doesn't like me, does she?"

"Oh, she likes you fine. That's her problem. I don't think her . . . impoliteness worries you much."

He shrugged. "Hardly. She's being protective, and I can understand that. I won't hurt you, Susan."

She didn't answer for a moment. "I believe you."

His fingers tightened around hers in acknowledgement of her trust. Emotion welled up inside her.

"Your grandmother said something about visiting her sister."

Susan grinned slyly. Her grandmother's sister was . . . different. "Yes. Tomorrow. We won't be at the beach."

"I see."

He sounded so disappointed, she thought. Her grin widened. "Would you like to go with us?"

"I wouldn't be intruding?"

"No. Actually, you'd be company for me, if you wouldn't mind going."

He smiled. "I'd love to."

"Good."

He dropped her off at home with an almost brotherly kiss. Almost. Susan admitted there had been a definite touch of passion in the way his lips shaped themselves to hers.

Lettice was waiting just inside the door for her. Her arms were folded across her chest, and she was frowning.

"Well? Did you talk to him?"

"Oh, sure," Susan said blithely, carting the basket back into the kitchen.

"And?"

"And he's going with us tomorrow."

"Susan!"

"Grandmother!" Susan parroted back. "Your sister will be good for his soul."

Lettice paused, then chuckled. "Good point."

"I thought so."

When he joined them the next morning, Susan warned Remy that her great-aunt was unusual. He got his first inkling of just how unusual when they turned into the long shell drive of St. Anne's by-the-Sea in Loveladies, a seaside town about thirty miles from Atlantic City.

St. Anne's was a retreat for nuns.

He tried to accept the idea that Lettice's sister was a nun. He couldn't.

"Your sister is a nun?" he asked baldly.

"Yes," Lettice said from where she sat in regal splendor in the backseat of the Mercedes. "Eleanor gave up the world fifty years ago, along with her name. I've never quite forgiven her. She's now Sister Stephen Philomena."

Remy swallowed hard as his brain resurrected visions of tall, stern women in black habits with long, hard rulers. He had gone to parochial school only until the sixth grade, but he'd never forgotten the experience. Sister Marie Matilde had been the worst. She was probably here, waiting for him. . . .

Susan patted his knee. "It's not that bad, Remy."

He glared at her for taking such liberties in the presence of a convent. Granted, he might have had a running image since yesterday of the two of them twisting and turning with desire among the dunes, but that had vanished the moment they turned in the drive.

"Yes, it is that bad, Susan. I was the worst kid in the parish. Nuns have a sixth sense about those things."

Susan and her grandmother laughed.

Out of the car, Remy walked ever more slowly toward the front entrance. The large Victorian clapboard building was set on a small promontory overlooking the sea. It was surrounded by low dunes, and he fought the urge to lose himself in the seagrass. He couldn't even look at Susan. If he did, he'd lust in his heart, and this was no place to indulge in that pleasure.

Once inside, he sat gingerly on the edge of a settee as they waited in the sitting room for Susan's great-aunt. He cursed under his breath, then cursed again for cursing. It was amazing, he thought, to have this kind of reaction when he considered what he did for a living. Still, he couldn't help it. No one who went to parochial school could.

He wondered what the sister would be like, then shuddered at the thought of *two* Lettices. Two of them, regal and domineering, staring at him with that direct look that seemed to go through a person. Worse, Lettice's sister had taken the names of martyrs. He shuddered again, thinking of what Sister Stephen Philomena would be like.

A nun in a white habit entered the sitting room, and Remy stared at her. She had Lettice's features, but she was different. Very different. There was an aura of purity about her, as if she'd been born centuries too late. A sweet innocence radiated from the small woman. Not naïveté, he thought, automatically standing out of respect. Her smile of indulgence said she was quite aware of the world and its foibles, yet she was untouched by them.

Sister Stephen Philomena conjured visions of medieval cloisters and a world dictated by devotion. She was about as far from Lettice Kitteridge as one could get.

And Sister Marie Matilde.

Remy relaxed as greetings were exchanged. He was almost comfortable, watching a subdued Lettice kiss her sister. Susan smiled at him, and he vowed to shoot her when they got out of there. She could have warned him.

"And this is Susan's friend," Lettice said, "Mr. Remy St. Jacques. He's visiting the area from Canada."

"It is kind of you to accompany my sister and niece, Mr. St. Jacques," Sister Stephen said.

"It is my honor." He meant it.

Sister Stephen smiled. At first he was pleased, but then he noticed her smile held an odd sadness. He couldn't help feeling she was somehow disappointed in him, as if she were aware of the lies and half-truths his life demanded of him. As if she knew how he had deceived Susan . . . knew about how he was seducing his way into her trust. As if she had divined it all in an instant.

He felt an invisible punch land squarely in his stomach. Guilt assailed every corner of his being at what he was doing with Susan.

Sister Stephen Philomena might not know, but he did.

And he hated himself for it.

Five

It was too much for Susan. She stood up and said, "I'm sorry, but I need to go outside."

"Are you all right, child?" Sister Stephen asked.

Susan wanted to scream that no, she was not all right, that her guilt had surfaced tenfold, that if she were to sit there any longer she'd explode.

She drew in a deep breath. "I'm all right, really. It's just a little stuffy in here."

Lettice raised her eyebrows. "But it's only seventy—"

Sister Stephen laid a hand on Lettice's arm. "Of course, Susan. Go on."

As she left the room, Susan couldn't look at Remy.

Stepping outside was like being released from torture. She leaned against the car, wondering how one small woman could wreak so much mental havoc. But that was what Sister Stephen had done.

She had felt . . . unclean under the sister's saintly eye. All of her lying and evasions of the past years had been laid bare for everyone to see. She knew she had been turning a blind eye to Ross's corruption. Her grandmother worried about Remy being a cheat and a gigolo, but Susan knew she was the one deceiving him, deceiving everyone.

Five minutes in the retreat and she'd realized how much she had been suppressing her conscience over Ross. What he was doing was wrong. If she had any honor at all, she would stop the corruption . . . now.

"Are you okay?"

Remy's voice was gentle and concerned, and when Susan looked up she saw a like expression on his face. No matter what he might be, *she* wasn't being fair to him. Granted, she was honestly attracted to him, but she was using him as an excuse not to deal with Ross.

She grimaced. "I'm okay."

He nodded, then folded his arms across his chest and lounged against the car. He was close enough for her to feel his body heat. She had her hands braced on either side of her, and her fingers were just a scant inch from his hip. Her blood slowed as the urge to move her hand quickened.

"You should have warned me about your great-aunt," he said in an aggrieved tone.

"What? And spoil the fun?" She actually laughed and was surprised that she did. She was silent for a moment, then added, "You know, I can't think of her as my great-aunt. She gave up all relationships when she 'left the world,' as Grandmother says."

"She does seem otherworldly." He grinned and leaned forward. "But so do you, especially when you attack me like you did yesterday. You sent me out of this world."

Her face heated. "You're back to normal."

He chuckled. "You just needed a jolt back to reality, *chère*."

Susan thought about her attack of conscience. It seemed she'd already received a jolt. Now she had to act on it.

"Susan?"

She mentally shook herself. "I'm sorry."

"Want to talk about it?"

She gazed at him. She only knew what he had told her and her grandmother about himself, and she couldn't honestly say it was all true. It would take a leap of faith to trust Remy St. Jacques.

Well, she thought. This was the place to do it.

"I . . . have a friend, a good friend who's doing something wrong." Having started, she realized it felt right to tell Remy. She took a deep breath and put the truth into words for the first time.

"*Wrong* is too polite. He's doing something criminal. Taking money, bribes for . . . I know I should stop him, but I can't. He helped me through some bad times. I can't forget that."

"I see."

She frowned at the coldness in his voice. Maybe he was able to think in more black and white terms than she.

"So you're torn between conscience and friendship?" he asked.

"Yes."

He drew in an audible breath and let it out slowly, then smiled. "I've been there. It's not easy, *chère*."

She relaxed slightly at the endearment. She must have imagined the cold tone before. "I've already figured that out. Unfortunately."

He took her hand. The warmth of his touch

surrounded her . . . then sent her senses spinning. Yesterday came roaring back to her mind—
his mouth on hers, the incendiary kiss, his hands
like fire on her skin.

A deep ache began in her belly and spread outward. She told herself this was not the place or
the time, but her wayward body refused to listen.

"Susan."

She forced herself to look at him . . . and saw
the same hunger in his eyes.

"Remy—"

"Oh, no," he interrupted, squeezing her hand.
"You got me in trouble yesterday with that."

She swallowed. "I only said your name."

"But it's the way you say it, *chère*. Drives me
to the brink."

The hot blush on her cheeks was almost pain-
ful, and she could only imagine how it must look.

Before she could say anything, though, Lettice
came outside, accompanied by Sister Stephen
Philomena. Remy dropped her hand like a hot
potato and straightened away from the car. Susan snorted in amusement. So much for flirting,
she thought.

"Are we ready?" Lettice asked.

"Very," Susan said.

Remy growled under his breath.

Sister Stephen kissed her cheek. "Have faith
and you will find your way through your troubles,
Susan."

Susan tried not to gape. Sister Stephen smiled,
love and faith shining out of her kindly eyes. Susan supposed she had been transparent earlier.
She smiled and hugged the woman. "Thank you. I
will."

Sister Stephen took Remy's hand and said something in a low voice to him. His eyes widened in surprise. Susan wondered what she had said, but it had been rapid and in French, too quick and too faint for her brain to sort out. Clearly Remy had understood, and he looked as chagrined as she felt.

"Now, don't berate the children, Lettice," Sister Stephen said after kissing the other woman's cheek.

"I do *not* berate!" Lettice exclaimed in a huff.

"Of course." Sister Stephen's eyes filled with amused tolerance. "She's agreed to leave you two be. Hold her to it."

"Yes, Sister," Remy said solemnly.

Susan chuckled, watching her grandmother turn toward the car, grumbling under her breath. It would serve Lettice right if they did.

He was back to normal.

Remy sighed happily, surrounded once again by half-naked tanning bodies on the beach. Having all those women around was reassuring on some subconscious level, but his attention was held by one, as always.

Susan was lying languorous and sublime next to him, and he admitted there was nothing like thoughts of sex to bring a man to his senses.

One sense anyway. The encounter with Sister Stephen had been disturbing, especially when she'd quietly told him to examine his soul. He had been bothered by that statement ever since.

And he had been bothered by what Susan had said when they'd been outside the retreat. Was the story about the "friend" really a friend . . . or her? Her brief explanation certainly fit what Ross had said. Still, she hadn't seemed guilty, as she might if she were the one doing something criminal. Instead, she had been more sad. And if it really was a friend, who was it? Who could evoke such a loyalty from her? He hated and envied such a man.

Still, she had taken him into her confidence. She was trusting him. Guilt at the way he was deceiving her surfaced, nearly smothering him. He forced it away. They would need that trust between them as he tried to help her out of whatever mess she was in. A little more time and a lot more trust and he would broach her on it.

Out of the corner of his eye he saw Lettice shift her beach chair back from the lengthening rays of sun invading the cabana.

Hiding a grin, he thought of the way Sister Stephen had pegged her. Lettice had grumbled all the way home the day before. When he'd glanced at Susan, he'd seen the same amusement, and the same thought that they would give Lettice a break that night. He had gone back to his motel for a lonely dinner, a lonely bed, and thoughts of honor. And thoughts of how he'd been lacking in any for a long, long time.

"Susan, we need to be going home early today," Lettice said.

Susan raised herself on one elbow, turning the upper half of her body toward Remy as she glanced back at her grandmother. Her breasts nearly overflowed her bandeau top. Remy resisted the urge to yank it away and take his fill of her. Definitely back to normal.

"But why?" Susan asked. "We got here only a short time ago."

"Because I've asked an old friend to dinner tonight."

Remy grinned at Susan, who grinned back.

"An old friend, eh?" Susan echoed. "Is he handsome? Is he sexy? Is he under ninety?"

"Yes, yes, and most definitely yes. Kippie Kenton's not forty yet."

Remy smothered a fit of laughter at the name.

"Kippie!" Susan exclaimed less graciously. "You've got to be kidding!"

Remy chuckled. "I don't think so, *chère.*"

"He's just a *friend*," Lettice snapped, emphasizing the last word. "Really, Susan, what do you think I am?"

"An absolute knockout no man could resist?"

"I might have bought that if you hadn't sounded like you were trying to convince yourself more than me," Lettice said in a quelling voice.

Remy laughed. He stopped laughing, though, at Lettice's next words.

"I think you'll find Kippie Kenton very intriguing, Susan."

White-hot jealousy burned through Remy. Lettice couldn't have been any more transparent in her matchmaking attempt if she had tried. It was clear Sister Stephen had no influence over this one.

"I'm sure I will," Susan said calmly.

Jealousy immediately turned to anger.

"Remy," Susan went on, "would you like to join us tonight?"

He blinked at the abrupt change. "I . . . yes."

Susan smiled, almost gratefully.

He smiled back, relieved. She wasn't interested in whoever her grandmother had in mind for her, and he was damn happy about that.

Lettice glared at the two of them. "When are you going back to Montreal, Remy?"

He shrugged. "I have some time coming to me."

"You've got more than that," Lettice muttered just loud enough for him to hear. But she didn't uninvite him.

He was elated, then worried. Clearly Lettice thought she had a winner.

That night, as Remy sat across the table from Kippie Kenton, he decided the man was a winner . . . of the jerk-of-the-year award.

He supposed a woman would find Kenton's blond good looks appealing. Personally he thought the man looked like a washed-out chicken. And his tenor voice had droned on throughout dinner with one Kippie Kenton accomplishment after another. It was still droning, like a drill in a sadistic dentist's office.

"We put the boat out on the river and sculled up the Schuylkill for three miles. It was a quick burst for us. Olympic time, you know, Susan." Kippie smiled smugly.

"Is there any other kind?" Susan murmured. Lettice had very obviously seated her granddaughter next to Kenton. Susan looked sensational in a white sleeveless linen dress and black onyx jewelry. Remy alternated between vexation and pleasure at the very sight of her.

The jerk beamed at her. "I have never thought so. And coming back we cut the time even more. People told us we were just what the Olympic rowing team needed in eighty-four, but Cyril and I weren't interested in all the races one has to enter beforehand to qualify for the team. I told them it was a very silly rule."

Silence fell for a moment before the three of them realized the man had actually shut up.

"How . . . too bad," Lettice said into the breach.

"It's a shame you can't stay for tomorrow, Kippie. The casino is holding a ceremony to hand over the proceeds from Côte d'Azur Night—"

"Really?" Kippie said in a very bored voice. "I've always thought casinos a waste of time."

Lettice smiled brightly. "Well, are we ready for dessert? Mamie has made raspberry torte."

"My favorite," Kippie said, completely oblivious to the embarrassment he had caused his hostess. "I remember the time Mother's cook substituted blueberries. An unpalatable mess. Mother was mortified."

The mouth was off and running again, Remy thought, suppressing a sigh. He glanced at Susan, who gave him a desperate look in return. Remy chuckled under his breath. His poor Susan. At least he had better manners than the purebred. He would not outstay his dubious welcome.

"I would love to stay for dessert, Lettice," Remy said, breaking into the monologue. "But I have to make several calls to Vancouver before the time difference gets much larger. I apologize for my rudeness."

Lettice stared at him, clearly surprised. A haunted look came over her face for an instant, then she smiled graciously. "We understand completely, dear."

He returned her smile, knowing she wasn't happy to be left with Motor-Mouth. Lettice Kitteridge was something.

"I'll walk you to your car," Susan said, jumping to her feet. "You'll excuse me, Kippie."

"Oh . . ." Kippie looked bewildered, as if he'd never lost an audience before. The look lasted half a second, then he was off and running again. "Do you have interests in Vancouver? I once owned a timber company out of that area, but the environmental restrictions were cutting into the profits terribly. . . ."

Remy laughed dryly and walked to the head of the table. "Thank you for having me," he said, and kissed Lettice's cheek. "The lobsters were wonderful." Sotto voce, he added, "You can do better than this for Susan."

Lettice harrumphed and waved him away in rueful resignation. She didn't even look disturbed that Susan was joining him.

Outside, Susan gave a huge sigh. "I'll kill her."

Remy laughed and put his arm around her. "It wasn't that bad, *chère*."

"Kippie Kenton is a talking Chinese water torture." She shuddered. "I *will* have a nice long talk with my grandmother."

"At least get her to bring in better boyfriend material."

"I don't need one, Remy."

He smiled to himself at the veiled admission that she didn't need a man because she already had one. She was right there. He was too wrapped up in her, and he knew it. He liked her next to him like this, casual and intimate at the same time.

"I wish you didn't have to go," she said when they reached his car. It was parked behind Kenton's Rolls coupe.

His male ego swelled a bit, and he sneered at the Rolls under cover of darkness. Much as he wanted to stay, he'd probably kill Kippie Kenton if he did.

Still . . .

"I could delay it long enough for a drive," he suggested.

She glanced back at the house. "I would be very bad just to leave."

"And why do I think you are about to be a very bad girl, *chère*?"

"Because I am. Get in."

She slipped away from him and hurried around to the passenger side. Remy unlocked the driver's door, got in, and reached over to unlock the passenger side.

She was inside the nondescript Chevy before he could blink. The expression on her face could only be described as naughty. Remy loved it.

"Poor Lettice is still stuck with the Talking Torture," he said. "Shall we rescue her too?"

She was silent for a long moment. "Naaa."

"I thought not." He started the car, and they drove off giggling like a couple of teenagers breaking curfew.

Neither said much while he drove, both seeming to prefer to listen to the radio.

Awareness slowly pervaded the car's interior. Remy had been expecting it when she agreed to the drive. This was a stolen moment away from Lettice, away from the lying and misdirections of the life he was leading.

A stolen moment. Remy tightened his fingers around the steering wheel. He'd turn it into hours and to hell with the cost.

Susan absently watched the scattered people on the sidewalk as they cruised along the avenue. Remy's presence overwhelmed her, filling her senses. Sensuality flowed through her in time to the smooth and powerful rhythm of Steve Winwood's voice on the radio. She was being seduced without being touched. Like a drug, the moments alone were a growing need.

This wasn't a distraction any longer. She knew that. After their visit to the retreat, the war inside her had been slowly ebbing away. She would call Ross, talk to him first to give him the chance to do the right thing. She owed him that.

The car turned away from people and bright lights toward the bay side and the dunes. Susan said nothing, allowing herself to be filled with the moment. Her grandmother could drain the world of Kippie Kentons, and it wouldn't change what was happening inside her. She wanted Remy.

He stopped the car at the end of a deserted road. The radio shut off automatically, bringing a loud silence. Neither of them got out of the car.

"I didn't think you were ready to go back yet," he said.

Susan drew in a slow, deep breath and turned to him. His face was shadowed, but she felt his gaze unwavering on her. "I wasn't."

He reached for her as she leaned toward him. His mouth was hot fire on hers this time. She opened for it, taking in the heat. Her tongue swirled around his in a never-ending duel. His hands were sure and deft on her back, his embrace crushing her breasts against his hard chest. Whatever concerns she might have about him faded in his arms. She almost didn't care if she was being a fool, but she knew she wasn't. Lettice could worry and parade a string of men before her. But Lettice hadn't found the core of honor in Remy. She hadn't cared to look closely enough. Her granddaughter had.

Remy cupped her breast, and all thoughts flew out of her head. Desire rocked her, and she moaned into his mouth. His thumb rubbed insistently across her nipple until it was hard and aching.

She dug her fingers into his shoulders, not caring that she was clinging to him.

The front buttons of her dress seemed to fall away on their own. In the sensual haze she hadn't noticed Remy's fingers working them loose, only that his hand was on her bare skin. His touch sent more shock waves through her already overloaded body.

He lifted his head. She slowly opened her eyes to find him staring at her.

"You feel like satin."

His eyes were glazed with passion, and she shuddered as he caressed her in wonder. He lowered his head to her breasts, branding first one, then the other with his tongue. The throbbing deep inside her grew, the rhythms pulsing through through her. Her breath came quick and short.

He tasted her endlessly, until she could stand it no longer. She pulled his mouth up to hers again, giving him her passion and absorbing his.

Her fingers found their way inside his shirt, tangling the whorls of silky hair on his chest. The beach had held frustrating hours of keeping herself from reaching out and touching him this way. His skin was hot, and she could feel the hard muscles underneath, tensing.

She moved, restless, even as his hand slipped beneath her dress. His fingers spread across the inside of her thigh. She groaned when they slid, slowly, lightly, along her sensitive flesh.

Hands and mouths traveled in a sensual exploration, touching, tasting, absorbing, insuring that this was no fantasy. There was a wildness inside her threatening to burst out of control, yet remaining in control because they were in the car. She could give in to all the sensations he created, knowing this was not the time or place for more. She sensed the same knowledge in him.

That reality eventually surfaced, and they slowly cooled their passion in a quiet embrace.

"You'll be the death of me, *chère*," he finally murmured, nuzzling her throat.

Susan laughed contentedly. There was a satisfaction in the dissatisfaction of the moment. "My grandmother will probably kill us both."

"It would be worth it."

She smiled, knowing she could stay there like that. In the next moment she sighed, knowing they had to go back.

"Do you think we're too old to be necking like teenagers?" she asked.

"Hell, no."

"I didn't think so either."

It was all too soon when they reluctantly broke apart and drove back to the house in an easy silence. Kippie's Rolls was gone.

"Come with us to the casino tomorrow," Susan whispered after he kissed her thoroughly under the lit porch light.

He kissed her jawline. "I already planned to."

It took two more kisses before the desire was brought under control. Susan stepped inside to the dark foyer, Remy's hands slipping away from her. She shut the door behind her, then turned and watched him through the stained glass inset until his shadow descended the porch steps and blended with the night. She sighed.

"That's what I thought."

She jumped and spun around. Lettice was standing on the threshold of the dining room, and Susan realized she'd been there for quite some time.

"You scared me half to death, Grandmother."

Lettice flipped on the foyer light. Susan blinked against the sudden brightness.

"You scared *me* when you disappeared like that."

Susan smiled sweetly. "He was *your* guest, not mine. Thank goodness."

"All right, so he wasn't perfect—"

"No more, Grandmother," Susan broke in, her repressed anger surfacing. "I mean it."

Lettice eyed her for a long moment. "I called my lawyer a few days ago. I asked him to check on our friend, Mr. St. Jacques."

Susan didn't move.

Lettice was silent for a moment. "Nothing."

"Nothing?" Susan echoed.

"Nothing!" her grandmother snapped, sounding put out. "Nothing extraordinary, nothing out of place. Just an ordinary man."

Susan relaxed, shrugging. "What did you expect? We found him, remember?"

"I still maintain he's not ordinary."

Susan suppressed a vigorous nod of agreement. "Stop worrying, Grandmother. And no more Kippie Kentons, please!"

Lettice smiled ruefully. "I'd forgotten what a pill he could be."

They laughed together.

The ceremony at the casino was more for the press than for the charity. Lettice smiled through all of it, her grin widening even more when the famous entrepreneur handed her a sizable check. The media's cameras flashed and whirred. Standing to the right of her grandmother on the boardwalk, Susan grinned at Remy, who looked down at her and chuckled. Lettice had been charitable to him when he'd arrived at the house, although she had grumbled under her breath when he'd kissed her granddaughter.

Poor Lettice didn't quite know what to do with Remy, Susan thought. Neither did she, as a matter of fact.

But she did know where to start rebuilding her life. When they got home after the ceremony, she excused herself and went into the den.

Forcing away the panic, she picked up the telephone and dialed a very private number.

The telephone rang twice before it was answered.

At the sound of Ross's voice, Susan automatically hung up.

She stared at the telephone, astonished at her own actions. She knew she had to talk to him. But clearly the telephone wasn't the way to do it.

She set her jaw, determined to ease her conscience and take herself out of this limbo. Something was happening between her and Remy. Something she didn't want spoiled by her dilemma with Ross. She would have to have a conversation with the man to achieve that.

Somehow, some way.

Six

They weren't going to the beach.

Remy stepped on the Chevy's brakes and pulled in behind a car parked two houses down from the Kitteridge home. A cab waited out in front of the Kitteridges, the driver holding the door open for his passenger. Remy leaned forward on the steering wheel and stared at the two women standing on the shell walkway.

Susan said something to her grandmother, then kissed her on the cheek. As she walked to the cab, her movements barely disturbed the straight fall of her skirt. *Somber* and *power* were the two words that came to his mind as he studied her gray suit. He frowned. If Susan were going to a funeral, wouldn't Lettice be going too? Lettice's sky-blue top and slacks told him that wasn't the case.

He had arrived early that day. He admitted he hadn't been able to stay away from her a minute longer. Obviously Susan didn't have the same problem. And wherever she was going, *no one* had told him about the change in plans.

A sick feeling started in the pit of his stomach, even as the hairs on his arms rose. His instincts began to sound an alert. Where the hell was she going?

She got into the cab, and it immediately rolled away from the curb. Remy checked his gas gauge and mentally calculated the funds in his pocket. Both his gas tank and wallet were full, a habit born out of precaution.

He waited for Lettice to go inside, then drove off, catching up with the cab around the corner. He kept five cars back, far enough to look innocent but close enough to keep his quarry in sight. The cab pulled into the train station, and he watched Susan walk inside. He had never seen her dressed for business before. He wanted to strip away the power suit and find the woman he knew underneath. His Susan.

But *his* Susan hadn't said a word about this trip. Something told him she didn't intend to either. He parked in the station lot and was inside the terminal a few minutes later.

He spotted Susan almost instantly at the ticket counter. Glancing up at the track board, he saw that the only train leaving within the half hour was a gamblers express returning to Philadelphia. It had to be the one she was taking. He knew from the information Ross had given to him that the Kitteridge family had lived in Philadelphia for generations. Maybe Susan was visiting relatives. Maybe she was running an errand for Lettice. There were a hundred explanations for her taking a train somewhere, all of them innocent. Remy hoped one of those explanations was the right one.

He was dressed in denim cutoffs, a plaid shirt, and a pair of high-tops. Not conspicuous for a summer resort, but not inconspicuous either in the sparsely populated lobby. Cursing his appearance, he slipped on his sunglasses and pulled his baseball cap lower on his brow.

Fifteen minutes later he managed to get on the train just as the conductor called, "All aboard." He was three cars back from Susan.

"Whew! Just made it," he said, smiling at the conductor. He had made sure to get on the same car as the man. He braced himself as the train lurched into motion, then said ruefully, "I didn't have a chance to get a ticket . . ."

The conductor smiled and waved a hand. "When I collect the others, I'll issue you one then. Hope you won enough to cover it, son."

Remy grinned. "Me too."

Confusion tormented Remy the whole way to Philadelphia's 30th Street Station. Images of Susan responding to his kisses with incredible passion filled his mind. He thought that she would have told him beforehand where she was going . . . but she hadn't.

The bigger crowds at the Philadelphia station provided better cover, and he was grateful for it, especially when Susan did not take the stairs to the street level. Instead, she headed for another track. He cursed under his breath when he read the track board.

She was going to Washington.

The second train trip was as uneventful as the first, and by the middle of the afternoon they were in the city. His taxi driver didn't even blink when he showed him a badge and told him to follow another cab. It was easy in Washington's horrendous traffic to stay back while keeping Susan in sight. Nobody appreciated the snail's pace better than an undercover man tailing his quarry, Remy thought with black humor.

Every instinct told him something was horribly wrong.

His consternation grew when it became clear her taxi was headed toward Georgetown. He stared in astonishment as it turned down a familiar street and stopped in front of a familiar town house. Slinking back in the seat, he told his driver to continue on. He turned around in time to see Susan walking up the steps of Ross Mitchelson's home.

Remy faced forward again and gazed unseeing at the car ahead of them.

He had been betrayed.

Fear overwhelmed her every sense as she stared at the door. Every instinct was screaming at her to get out, to get away before she was seen. She knew what had seemed so right a day before was very wrong.

She spun around just as her cab was pulling away from the curb. "Wait!"

She raced down the steps and hurtled back into the taxi. Relief washed through her for a second.

"Wasn't it the right address?" the driver asked.

"I . . . was mistaken." Her hands started shaking. She had to get away before Ross saw her—if he hadn't seen her already. Her heart pumped sickening horror along her veins. She said the first thing that came into her head. "The Washington Monument, please."

The driver shrugged and eased the cab into traffic, clearly not surprised by odd passenger requests.

The cab driver took her to more than one point of interest in the nation's capital. She sat unthinking during the entire two-hour excursion. Or rather, she thought too much. None of her thoughts, however, were coherent.

Later on the train home, she was ready to deal with what had happened in front of Ross's house.

Plain old fear for survival, she told herself. She understood now why she had run after that party at Trevor's, after she had gone out for fresh air and had seen Ross exchanging money with that senator's aide. She might have thought it was a personal loan—only it was too much money, and more than once she had seen the senator's aide huddled together with someone whom she knew was with an unfriendly government's embassy. The Washington community was a small one, and she'd been part of it for a long time.

She'd put two and two together and come up with a shocker. The incident had been too open, too confident, as if Ross had no fear of discovery. That was what had scared her so much, sending her straight out of Washington to the first safe haven she could get to. And it was what had kept her scared for so long after.

Ross *was* an enormously powerful man. And he was something else she hadn't wanted to admit: ruthless. She knew some of the political happenings in the world had the Company behind them. Ross was the Company. She was also aware that powerful men did not like to lose their power, and ruthless men went to any length to keep that from happening. She had nearly forgotten that earlier. If she had walked into his home and discussed what she had seen, it would have been the worst mistake of her life.

Certainly the stupidest, she admitted with a grimace of disgust. She had been blinded by the honor of friendship. Now she could see.

At the moment Ross didn't know what she had seen. And she didn't know what he thought of her sudden exodus from Washington. Perhaps that she'd just up and quit. She wondered how many people had done that and hoped it wasn't unusual. But her bigger problem was whether he had seen her outside his house.

Susan groaned at the thought, imagining what he could guess from that. Still, logic told her she hadn't been looking out the window or even been home at that precise moment, so the odds were still in her favor. After all, she hadn't called first. One part of her brain had been working, thank goodness.

The one good thing she had done was confront her indecision about Ross. She knew that whatever she might owe the man, her silence wasn't a payment of the debt. Unfortunately, who to go to with her information was her new stumbling block. She didn't know the hierarchy beyond Ross.

Okay, she thought, so she had a little researching to do there. In the meantime, she would write down everything she knew as insurance, if something "unforeseen" should happen. She gritted her teeth at her rising fear and told herself to think about something else.

Trying to relax, she flipped through the copy of the day's *Washington Post* that she had bought at the station newsstand. She stopped at the entertainment page when she caught sight of a familiar face. The photograph was of her grandmother accepting the charity check. She could just distinguish herself and Remy in the background crowd.

She remembered the night they had sneaked away from her grandmother's dinner party. Remnants of passion shuddered through her even now, and she closed her eyes. Her breathing slowed. The need to experience that passion again, and more, much more, began to overtake her sanity. He wasn't even there and he could evoke this kind of response from her.

She might not have resolved Ross, but Remy was definitely becoming a different kind of solution.

One she needed desperately.

"You didn't check in earlier as we'd arranged."

Remy's hold on the telephone receiver tightened. "Yes, I know. I . . . was delayed."

He waited for Ross to comment about Susan's visit to Washington. If he did, the odds were it meant the visit was an innocent one. Remy hoped.

"I figured her and her grandmother," Ross said, "are on the social whirl there, trying to look ordinary. No doubt they keep you busy."

Ross's voice held a touch of resentment and sarcasm. But no mention of the visit, Remy thought. His blood chilled ominously in his veins.

Ross went on. "My . . . friend tells me the pass will come any day. They think she'll be an asset to them, so they're sending 'Peter' to take delivery. That's been the delay. Peter's been busy elsewhere. You remember Peter."

"I remember him."

How could he forget the man who had turned three other Company agents, Remy thought. He had almost gotten the elusive Peter once. He'd like to try again. The only problem was that Peter had been inactive for several years, and Ross should know that.

Remy frowned. This didn't feel like a Peter operation, but rather that the name was being used as a lure for him. A kind of sleight of hand that he wouldn't be able to resist.

"Stick very close now," Ross added.

Remy smiled grimly. "Sure," he said, and hung up the phone.

That sense of a lure was very strong, he mused. If Ross had been lying this time about Peter, and Remy was almost positive he was, then what else had he lied about? And Susan going to his home as she had . . . what had she lied about? What were the two of them in together?

Remy froze. He had been sent to her. By Ross. And now Ross had told him to stay close.

The way Susan heated at his touch came back to haunt him. Her mouth was fire and ice, and a man could lose himself in her passion. He almost had. He damn well couldn't have gotten any closer. Maybe what he had seen today was a warning of the dangers of mixing business with desire.

Especially in his line of work.

"I didn't have to cover for you," Lettice said. "He didn't show up."

Susan paused as she took off her jacket, then continued the process. "Oh?"

"Yes." Lettice pointed to a vase of freesias, daisies, and bachelor buttons set on the foyer table. "He sent those in apology. It was business, so our Remy says. Same as you."

Not quite, Susan thought. She touched a stalk of the small striped freesias, pleased by his thoughtfulness. The attached card said only that he had had a business emergency and he was "very sorry to have missed our ritual at the beach." She smiled at the explanation, then stretched to dispel the sudden tiredness in her body. It had been a long and traumatic day.

"Grandmother, when are you going to admit that you like Remy?"

"I never said I didn't," Lettice said defensively. She hugged her robe more tightly to her body. "I'm just concerned, Susan. He just doesn't seem to be what he says."

"I think," Susan said slowly, "that he is quite unique."

Lettice grumbled something unintelligible.

"How nice of you to agree," Susan quipped, walking toward the darkened kitchen. She was desperate for something to drink.

Lettice followed. "So are you going to tell me what today was all about?"

"I already did. Business." She turned on a light, then took a pitcher of ice cold lemonade out of the refrigerator.

"Missy," Lettice exclaimed as Susan poured herself a large glass, "you went out of here like the hounds of hell were about to swallow you, and you came home like a prisoner just released from a twenty-year jail term. That's a lot more than business!"

"Grandmother, please." Susan took a long swallow of the lemonade, and the tart sweetness was rejuvenating. "It was personal business. There are other people involved, and I won't discuss it." She smiled gratefully at her grandmother. "You've been very patient with me, especially after the way I descended on you. I can only ask that you be patient with me now."

"Damn!"

Susan chuckled. Her grandmother always liked to be in the know.

"I can't exactly complain at your honor," Lettice said. "Will you be leaving now that your trouble is over?"

She was taken aback by her grandmother's assumption that she'd resolved her problems. She wondered if she *should* leave. But where could she go? She might know now that she could never go to Ross, but she still had to do something.

"Would you mind if I stayed a little longer?" she asked. "I won't be going back to Washington."

Lettice smiled and hugged her. "Stay as long as you like, dear."

Susan thought of Remy . . . of the way his touch felt so right . . . of the way she felt so alive when she was with him.

She'd stay forever if she could.

"I'm sorry I wasn't here yesterday. It was a family matter I had to take care of for Grandmother."

Remy nodded nonchalantly as he took the picnic basket from her. Lettice was walking ahead, actually allowing them a measure of privacy.

He gritted his teeth against a surge of anger at Susan's lie, then said in an extremely gentle tone, "I understand, *chère.*"

Susan took a deep breath and smiled at him. She looked far too happy with the world to suit him.

"I missed you, Remy," she said, leaning close to him.

He tightened his fingers around the basket's handle until the thin strands of polished wicker cut into his skin. "I missed you. I did have some unexpected business too."

"Your flowers of apology were lovely . . . and your card was quite innocent." She sent him an intimate sidelong glance.

He had thought long and hard about his options the night before. Eventually he had realized he couldn't just walk out without arousing suspicions. And whatever was going on was not what Ross said. That worried him. His instincts much preferred he find out exactly what was going on. He felt as if he had all the puzzle pieces, and now only had to fit them into place. Until then he didn't know what options he had in this game.

He suppressed the urge to strangle her for the torture she was putting him through. Damn her, what was she doing? What was she? He couldn't believe the change in her, and it was more confusing than ever. She was so damn happy, as if the weight of the world had been lifted from her shoulders. What had happened during her talk with Ross to change her? Had she given back the documents she'd supposedly stolen? Not according to Ross. Had she come to an arrangement with him over her "activities"?

He had believed she was a wronged innocent—until yesterday. Now he didn't know what to believe.

Her every movement, her every look, her every smile, even the very scent of her had his blood surging with anger . . . and desire. By the time they reached their spot on the beach, he was boiling with his emotions.

"I'm going in for a swim," he announced after dropping his things in a pile. He peeled off his T-shirt and flipped it on top of his crumpled towel.

Lettice stared at him from inside the cabana. He knew this completely broke his usual routine of baking on the sand first, then going in the water. He didn't care. Turning, he jogged toward the ocean.

"Hey!" Susan said, catching up with him. "You forgot me."

He set his jaw and took a deep breath. "Sorry. I didn't think you were ready yet."

"You didn't ask."

Shrugging, he waded into the surf, the first waves smacking into his body. The chill of the summer Atlantic was a needed shock to his system. He dove into the next wave, cutting through it cleanly, then surfacing again in the waist-high water.

Susan surfaced next to him.

"Feel better?" she asked, grinning at him.

No, he thought. He felt worse, because he didn't know what to think about her. He was back to square one with a vengeance.

She gazed at him. Her eyelashes were beaded with water, turning her blue-green eyes into dazzling jewels. Her bathing suit clung to her, outlining every intimate detail of her breasts. The bodice exposed so much cleavage it was almost indecent, and her nipples were tightly puckered beneath the fabric.

"Remy?" she whispered.

He grabbed her and pulled her to him. His kiss was harsh and demanding, nearly forcing her lips apart for his tongue. Her skin was like cool satin, and he dug his fingers into her back in an effort to meld her with his own flesh. He didn't care that people were staring at them. He wanted to transfer all his fury into her, to make her see that whatever she was up to was wrong.

But slowly the kiss changed to the rightness of

passion. Need overcame anger until he could no longer deny it. He buried his face in her shoulder, just holding her tightly.

She stroked his arms. "Tell me what happened."

He kissed her cool flesh, then said, "I lost . . . an account yesterday."

"The Vancouver one?"

He closed his eyes for a long moment, then lied. "Yes. It ticked me off. I'm sorry I took it out on you."

"You didn't. You were just quiet." She chuckled. "Grandmother is probably having a fit at our . . . impropriety."

He smiled wistfully, then raised his head. "Then let's be improper again."

His mouth covered hers. The kiss held a tenderness that left him no hope. He couldn't stop this no matter what happened. He was obsessed.

The waves pulled them under.

Seven

For the next five days Susan couldn't stop smiling. She smiled at the old ladies gossiping under a circle of striped umbrellas.

She smiled at the mothers sunning themselves and indulgently watching their children cover themselves with sand.

She smiled at the people strolling the boardwalk, smiled at the souvenir shops, smiled at the rain when it poured from the normally blue skies.

She smiled at everyone and everything. She was retired . . . and there was Remy.

When Susan emerged from the little knickknack shop, hoping to see Remy and the car, she was still smiling. There had to be a thousand souvenir shops along the Jersey shore, and she and Remy had explored every one of them on that rainy day. In fact, she could have sworn they'd been in this one twice. And the porcelain cottage she had bought for her grandmother had been in every shop so far.

She still didn't know who to tell about Ross, the

aide, and the money, but it had been a tremendous relief to realize she had made a decision. As each day had passed uneventfully, her underlying fears had lessened, allowing her to think. And to write. She had laid it out on paper and put that in a safe deposit box at a local bank. Directions for opening it were sent to her lawyer. She had been lighthearted ever since, even as she mentally went over lists of government people she knew who were powerful enough to take on Ross. She had several possibilities through her family connections, but she didn't know where their allegiances lay concerning Ross. She sensed she had only one chance to get out of this in one piece.

She realized she'd been standing on the curb for several minutes and Remy was nowhere in sight. She glanced up and down the street, but didn't see his Chevy. Cars were lining the curb, every parking meter taken in the cold, drizzly weather. The traffic was continually moving, though, at a fast pace. Remy had had to park in the lot across the street. Figuring he must still be getting the car, she decided to walk over and meet him to save time. Besides, they had a little talking to do. This rainy day was one of the few times they had been without their chaperone, and she had thought they would make the most of it. But Remy, for some strange reason, was avoiding being alone with her. Visiting every souvenir shop along the shore had been his idea.

There was a break in the traffic, and she stepped off the curb and began hurrying across the street. She heard the loud roar of a car engine being gunned to life and glanced around—just in time to see a car pull away from the curb.

It was coming straight at her.

• • •

He heard a scream. Susan's scream.

Remy slammed the car door shut and ran toward the noise. His internal warning bells went off like a twelve-alarm fire. He got to the street just in time to see Susan leap onto the sidewalk. Her eyes were wide with fear.

"Remy!"

"What? What is it? Are you okay?" He pulled her into his arms. She was shaking. He could feel the chill of her skin through her sweater.

"A car. It came right at me."

Fear jolted through him. He held her at arm's length, examining her. "Are you hurt, *chère*?"

"No." She swallowed visibly. "No. I'm okay. But the car . . . It came so close."

He glanced up and down the street, trying to find the car in question. Everything looked normal. Traffic along the street was busy, but moving continually. There was no suspicious car in sight.

He stopped a passerby, a middle-aged man who looked upstanding. "Excuse me, but my friend was almost hit by a car. Probably reckless kids. Did you happen to see what kind of car it was? We'd like to report it."

"I'm sorry," the man said sincerely, "but I didn't see anything out of the ordinary. Your friend just screamed and ran onto the sidewalk. Maybe she misjudged her distance."

"Thank you," Remy said, overriding Susan's squawk of protest. The man walked away.

"Dammit, I didn't misjudge anything," Susan said, angry. "He ought to see an optometrist!"

"Probably," Remy agreed, grateful that at least

she had stopped shaking. "Come on, let's go to the car."

Once they were seated in his car, he said, "Tell me what happened."

"I came out of the shop. You weren't around. I figured you must still be getting the car, and that I might as well meet you. I was crossing the street and this car just came out of nowhere, right at me." She shuddered. "I screamed and leapt out of the way."

"Where did it go? Did you see?"

"No," she snapped. "I was too busy running."

He clenched his teeth. "Susan, I'm just trying to find out what happened."

"I—I'm sorry." She rubbed her forehead. "I was so sure. That car just seemed to come straight at me."

He didn't know what to say to her. He had reached the street only seconds after she screamed. No car had stopped, and no car had been speeding away. No pedestrians had seemed interested. A couple of them had stared at Susan as if she had grown two heads. It sounded as if she herself were having doubts in retrospect.

But knowing what he knew about Susan . . .

"There are real accidents," he said. "That's why they're called that."

"I know. Remy, would you mind very much if we went home now?"

He smiled and started the car. "Of course not, *chère*."

They drove out of the parking lot and onto the street in silence. Remy kept his gaze as much on the parked cars and people they passed as on the traffic. He also glanced in his rearview mirror frequently. Nothing. Absolutely nothing.

He wondered what the game plan was now. Since he himself was back to square one in the game-plan department, he had no idea what was going on. Yet so far the plan hadn't included any "accidents." So far. That worried him.

He glanced over at her profile, still mesmerized by the curved fullness of her lips, by her skin like flawless porcelain, by her delicate bone structure and her hypnotic eyes. He was even more mesmerized by her warmth and graciousness, and by her mystery. Drawn to her in so many ways, he needed the truth from her. But he didn't know if he wanted to hear it.

"My cottage!" she suddenly exclaimed. "I must have dropped it."

He grinned at her. "Better the cottage than you *chère*."

Susan smiled in answer.

He turned his attention back to the road. The need to protect her was overwhelming; he was helpless to do anything else.

Even if it killed him.

"You're very quiet, Susan," Lettice said that evening as she and her granddaughter settled themselves on the veranda. "Did you and Remy have a fight? I hope not, or I might be forced to get Kippie back here."

Susan laughed. After what had happened that afternoon, she wouldn't have thought anything would make her laugh. She was still shaken, but the normal evening with her grandmother and Remy had restored her balance.

"I'm sure Kippie's not as bad as he seems," she

finally said, pushing the porch swing into motion. "Or you wouldn't have asked him."

Lettice shifted on the wicker chaise longue. "That's very gracious of you, Susan."

"I thought so."

"So did you two have a fight?"

"Try not to sound so eager, and no, we didn't. I'm just tired, I guess."

Remy emerged from inside the house, carrying a tray of tall frosted glasses. Susan smiled at him, taking pleasure in just watching him. He served her grandmother first, then her. After setting the empty tray on a vacant chair, he sat next to her, resting his arm casually along the back of the swing. The heat emanating from his body soothed her still-jangled nerves.

The moment they had returned home after her near accident, she had realized her mistake. She wasn't up to acting as if nothing had happened, and she wasn't up to her grandmother fussing over her. Remy had given her strength just by his presence. His calm and common sense had helped her to think beyond her initial shock. She had been so frightened by that car, but she must have frightened the driver even more. That was why he hadn't stopped. Or maybe he really hadn't seen her. Hindsight and logic told her she must have jumped to a wild conclusion. She acknowledged her judgment wasn't the most sound at the moment.

Doubts over her doubts surfaced again. She pushed them away, refusing to succumb to nonstop confusion. She wasn't hurt and that was what counted.

"I suppose," Remy said, breaking the silence, "I could talk about my track scores from high school."

He grinned at Lettice. "I was the slowest on the team, but I had great enthusiasm."

Lettice eyed him sourly. "Don't rub it in."

"Oh, no, ma'am. I wouldn't dream of it."

Susan stared at the two of them, surprised. It sounded as if the Kippie Kenton dinner had been for Remy's amusement rather than for her dubious benefit.

Her grandmother stood up. "I know when to retire gracefully. Good night."

Susan gaped as Lettice swept her inside.

"Your grandmother has more poise than the Queen of England," Remy said.

Susan nodded. "My grandmother taught poise to the Queen of England."

"I can believe it." He pushed the swing gently. "Feeling better now?"

"Mmm." She sighed, closing her eyes for a moment. When she opened them, she said, "It was nerves, I suppose. I must have sounded silly."

"No. Just shaken."

Neither said anything for a while, both content to sit together on the swing.

"Tell me about your family, Remy."

The swing halted abruptly. "My family?"

"Yes, your family." She laughed. "You know. Mother, father, sisters, brothers, etcetera. I just realized I really don't know a lot about your background. Just your work."

She knew she had deliberately suppressed her curiosity about him as a form of rebellion, because her grandmother had been *too* curious. But she *was* curious, now that she had time to be.

"But I've told you, *chère*."

"No, you haven't. Believe me, if I knew, I wouldn't be asking."

"But, Susan—"

"Remy." She made a face at him. "Now you're making me very curious."

He grimaced. "What do you want to know?"

"Everything." She snuggled closer to him, leaning into his side. His body held a warmth she craved, especially after today. "Do you have any brothers, sisters, aunts, or uncles? What about your parents? Past girlfriends? What other jobs did you have before this one with the chemical company? What college did you go to?"

He laughed. "Next you'll be asking my underwear size."

She ran her finger along the waistband of his jeans.

"I can guess."

He sucked in his breath. "This is not the place, chère."

"Makes it more fun." But she stilled her hands. "I suppose you're right. Now, about your family—"

"Too late." His fingers curved around her chin and he tilted her head back for his kiss.

The tender heat of his mouth made her forget everything except instant response. Her lips parted, tasting him, allowing him to taste her. He shifted her, pulling her against him. Her breasts were pressed to his hard chest as his hands swept across her back.

Whatever his reason for not wanting to be alone with her earlier, it wasn't loss of passion. Her curiosity could wait a little longer, she decided.

"Are you sure you're okay?" he asked when they finally and reluctantly broke apart.

"Mmm. I'm sure." She kissed the corner of his mouth, comforted by his concern.

"I hate to leave."

"I could sneak you past my grandmother." His hand brushed down the side of her breast, and she added breathlessly, "Especially when you do that."

"She'd catch us."

"It'd be worth a try."

He chuckled. "Are you trying to corrupt a nice boy like me?"

"Absolutely." She ran her tongue around his lips.

He shuddered. "I think I'm very corruptible."

He kissed her again, longer and more demanding. She wanted him, needed him. And she knew him, she thought as she tightened her arms around his neck. She knew he was a kind and caring man. He was an anchor in a world gone crazy. He touched the deepest core of her. And he was the man who sent her senses spinning into oblivion with just one look. That was what was important. Nothing else mattered.

When his mouth lifted from hers again, she realized she was in love with him.

She froze in amazement.

"What?" he asked, raising his head.

It was too new, too surprising to say aloud. Yet she felt as if the knowledge had always been there, just waiting for her to see it. She didn't know what to say to him, but she wasn't ready to tell him she loved him. She didn't know how he felt about her. And she wanted to explore it for herself first.

"Nothing." She stroked his cheek. "Nothing."

His fingers traced a pattern on her shoulder, and she relaxed back against him. She trusted him, trusted his judgment. It had been a long time since she had trusted any man.

Maybe it was high time she started to again.

Leaving was the last thing he wanted to do.

And so he hadn't.

Remy stared up at the house, the darkness wrapped around him as he stood under a massive oak tree.

He had been more scared than he cared to think at Susan's scream. She could have been hurt, and badly, and he hadn't been there to prevent it. In fact, he had been angry and confused with her when he had gone to get the car. That he could have lost her in something so simple as a car accident was unthinkable.

The day's heat was giving way to the cool night breezes. He listened to the low murmur of voices drifting from open windows, the hum of a car engine, and the occasional rattle of a trash-can lid. Tomorrow must be collection day. Nothing out of the ordinary reached his ears.

Despite his initial reaction, the incident with the car had played on his mind for the rest of the day. The more Susan had regained her equilibrium and come around to thinking it had been only a near accident, the more he had come to think it might not have been. His faith in his instincts, badly shaken by Susan's visit to Ross Mitchelson, was smoothing out. To his surprise, his original feelings about Susan hadn't changed. She still wasn't behaving as she should—if Ross's information about what was about to happen was true. She ought to be trying to get rid of him, not being playful. Or downright sexy. A man would stick like glue for any crumb she was offering.

The game wasn't being played exactly as he'd

thought it should, and that realization had thrown him. Somewhere, someone had all the moves plotted. He wondered now if that someone had just moved up to a deadly level.

He reminded himself that the information Ross was receiving and what he, Remy, was actually seeing were two entirely different things. He knew he should have told Ross his own doubts right at the beginning. Hell, he thought, he'd been telling himself that little ditty all along. The problem was he kept thinking "Remy knows best."

"And Remy doesn't," he muttered in a bare whisper. But he was beginning to wonder if Ross knew best. He was beginning to wonder just where Ross stood on the subject of Susan Kitteridge.

There was more to Susan than a question of innocence, however. Something about her reached the core of him, made him feel more alive than he had in a long time. For too long he had been sleepwalking in a bad dream. But Susan had awakened a gentle side in him. To see her so upset and shaken had shaken *him*. He had been worried about her, watching her all day with an intensity that surprised him. That kind of protective instinct was an indicator of his feelings for her.

Remy smiled to himself, thinking of another side of Susan. What she did to his body was remarkable. Denying himself her took tremendous strength. Strength he nearly lost on many occasions. Susan was a very dangerous woman. Not only did he want her, he needed her as he needed air. Any woman that had come before and any that would come after would never hold the intensity of Susan.

She was the perfect woman. And he was insane. He stared up at her bedroom window, lit by a soft light. A slender shadow passed across it, one he knew all too well. She was getting ready for bed. A bed without him.

He took a deep breath and shifted back against the tree. Insane or not, he wouldn't leave until he knew she was safe.

He couldn't.

Eight

She didn't want to leave the house.

"This is silly," Susan muttered, staring at the beach bag and cooler. She forced herself to pick them up. Remy would arrive in a few minutes for the daily trip to the beach. She'd feel better then.

Lettice came down the stairs, dressed in a voluminous striped burnoose, her face hidden by the wide cowl. "All ready," she announced cheerfully.

Susan shook her head. "Grandmother, why ever do you have a house in a beach resort? You must go home to Gladwynne looking more pale than when you came."

"I told you. I take the air." Lettice swept out the front door.

"The question is how," Susan said, hoisting the beach bag's straps onto her shoulder as she followed. "I certainly don't see any way it can get in."

"Susan, dear," Lettice said sweetly, "if you're not careful, I'll disinherit you."

"I bet you threaten all the grandchildren that way."

"And it never works." Lettice smiled. "I must say you are much more sassy than you were yesterday."

"I am," Susan said, realizing how relaxed she felt now. "Don't forget to wait for Remy. He's coming too."

"I know." Her grandmother fixed her with a stern look. "So when are you going to tell me what happened to bring you home hours before I expected you yesterday, and looking like a quivering mass of jelly besides."

Someday, Susan thought, her grandmother was going to be too shrewd for her own good. "I thought it was good manners for us to come back for dinner."

"In a pig's eye. If you think I'm swallowing that one, I suppose you'll have a bridge to sell me next."

"Grandmother, please."

Lettice was silent for a long moment. Since her expression was shaded by the burnoose, Susan had no idea what she was thinking.

"Just be warned," Lettice said at last, "you're getting my temper up. All this mystery is no good, Susan. And that includes Remy. It's very clear to me that there's something strong between you. Not only on your part, but also on his, I have to admit. As I said last night, I know when to surrender. I like Remy. It's just that he seems too *un*-ordinary for an ordinary man."

Susan smiled. "I know."

She also knew her grandmother wanted her to protect herself from being hurt. She could understand the need for it, but she had faith in Remy. And she had faith in herself that she wouldn't make the same mistake twice in her life.

Remy's car rolled to a stop at the curb, stopping the conversation. It was amazing, Susan thought as he got out of the car. She only had to look at him, at his rugged features, his long, lean body, and her blood was coursing through her veins at an Indy 500 rate. The discovery of love made him seem more good-looking, more sexy, more tender, and more caring. Every part of her being was focused on him, and everything else was a distraction.

She felt more secure with him around too. He possessed a lot of no-nonsense common sense. Cars deliberately coming at her seemed absurd and silly. If Ross were going to get rid of her, he'd surely be more subtle.

He came up the porch steps grinning and kissed her soundly on the lips. She flushed slightly when his gaze took in her blue bikini and matching hip-tied skirt. "I'll get arrested if I tell you how you look."

"Flatterer." She smiled back, the feel of his kiss still on her lips.

"And, Lettice, you look like a lovely extra from *Lawrence of Arabia*."

"And I was just thinking kindly of you," Lettice said. He only laughed, then turned back to Susan. "I suppose, *chère*, that you want me to carry all this junk."

"Naturally, since Grandmother wants *me* to carry all this junk."

"Can we go to the beach?" Lettice asked plaintively, then proceeded down the steps and across the shell walkway.

Remy took the "essentials" from Susan and they followed her grandmother, catching up to her at the sidewalk.

The trip to the beach took place without incident, and Susan sighed the moment her feet touched the already hot sand. She'd been more nervous than she thought.

"Feeling better?" Remy asked after they were settled on their towels and slightly out of Lettice's hearing distance.

"Yes."

"Good."

She refused to acknowledge that a crazy corner of her brain was holding on to the notion that the driver had come at her deliberately. Both she and Remy were lying on their stomachs, their shoulders almost touching. She could feel the heat of his body, which matched the heat of the sun beating down on her back. She concentrated on that.

He took her hand, his fingers warm and reassuring around her own. "Is your grandmother having another young friend over for dinner tonight?"

She chuckled. "No."

"Good. I'll pick you up at eight."

She nodded and smiled smugly to herself. She was determined that tonight would not end with dinner.

He leaned over and asked in a low voice, "Why do I think I should be nervous about that smile, *chère*?"

"Because you should."

He grinned, looking as un-nervous as a cat among the canaries.

Content with his reaction, she flipped onto her back to soak up more sun on her face and legs. She inhaled deeply of the fresh sea breezes and closed her eyes. Hearing a strangled moan, she opened one eye again. Remy was still lying on his stomach, his face oddly flushed.

"*Chère*, don't do that to a man without warning him first."

She took another deep breath and said, "Of course not."

"I'm going swimming." He was off the towel in less than a second and heading for the surf.

"Where's Remy going?" Lettice called out, pulling back the burnoose's hood.

Susan flipped over onto her stomach. "Swimming."

"I see." She tucked her head back into the recesses of the hood.

Susan had a feeling her grandmother saw very well. She didn't mind. She had fallen in love when she'd least expected it and the world was welcome to see it.

Tonight, she thought. Tonight was going to change her life.

It was the car screeching around the street corner that was hell-bent on changing her life.

They were on their way home from the beach, and Susan had stopped to shift the beach bag straps back onto her shoulder. In the split second that she saw the dark, nondescript car, she knew there was no mistake. It was coming straight at her as she stood in the middle of the small, normally quiet cross street.

"Susan!" Lettice screamed.

She was already moving, running for her life, but she knew she was too slow to outdistance the car barreling down on her. Remy was racing toward her in a hopeless attempt to save her. The roar of the car engine filled her ears as she put out her hand to stop him. He grabbed it and literally flung her out of the path of the speeding vehicle. For an awful moment it looked as if the spin of their bodies would put him right in front of the car's bumper, but the car whizzed harmlessly by. Susan, off balance and unable to regain her equilibrium, sprawled against the curb.

The car never stopped.

Remy was instantly at her side, lifting her slightly. She was too dazed to move herself. "*Chère* . . . the bastard . . . Susan, love, please . . . are you hurt? Did he hit you?"

His strong hand touched her limbs, and she forced herself to assess the damage. She felt bruised and battered and hurt, and there was a raw fire down her right leg, but she wasn't in any real pain.

"I'm okay. I think," she finally said, trying to smile. His hand tightened around hers. "Just my leg."

"You've got a bad scrape."

"Susan!" Lettice was on her knees next to her. Her grandmother's hands were shaking as they touched her face. They no longer looked beautifully manicured, but old and ravaged.

"I'm all right, Grandmother." She sat up—or tried to. Remy had to help her most of the way. She leaned against him, her whole body shaking with the effort. "Being flung into a gutter is absolutely wonderful. You ought to try it sometime."

Her grandmother smiled tearfully. "I think I'll pass. We better get you to a hospital—"

"No. I'm just shaken more than anything else. Help me up, Remy."

"Susan . . ." he began.

She struggled to get up on her own, not willing to argue the point but not willing to sit in the gutter either.

"Stubborn."

He helped her to her feet. She stood still for a long moment, waiting for the shaking to pass. She felt as if she'd been caught in a blizzard while wearing only a bikini. Her brain was on overload in the assessing department, but she thought she'd at least be able to stay upright.

"See?" she said. "The house is just up the street. If I don't make it, you can take me to the hospital."

Her grandmother looked more dubious than before. "We'll call the doctor. And we better call the police. It was a black car, mid-size, but I didn't see the license plates or even the driver. It was so fast. Did you see anything, Remy?"

"I was too busy square-dancing with Susan. Fortunately."

Susan said nothing. She began limping toward the house, the other two quickly joining her on either side. Remy put his shirt around her shoulders and took her right arm to support her. Lettice took her left, and Susan sensed that was more *in* support. She smiled reassuringly at her grandmother.

"The car . . . it came straight at you," Lettice said as if she couldn't hold the statement back any longer. "Right straight at you. It didn't even look as if the driver swerved at all. Why? Why would anyone do that?"

The shivers increased at the question. Susan realized that even though she'd thought it, she hadn't truly believed Ross would do such a thing. She would have to now. As soon as she was home, she thought, desperate to get there.

"I don't know why," Remy said slowly, answering Lettice.

Susan glanced up in time to see his piercing look. She knew he was remembering the near accident the day before.

"I'm sure it just seemed deliberate, Grandmother," she said, hoping Remy would understand she didn't want to upset her grandmother further.

"But he never stopped to see if you were all right!" Lettice exclaimed.

"Probably the driver was more scared than I. Could we hold the questions until we get me home?"

"Of course," Lettice said, gently squeezing her elbow.

She felt stronger physically by the time they reached the house. Her grandmother insisted, however, that she lie down on the sofa in the living room. Susan endured the fuss over her leg and herself in general, but when her grandmother finally left to call the doctor, she sighed with relief.

Remy smiled and sat down on the edge of the couch.

"I'm okay," she said. "It just makes Grandmother feel better to fuss like a mother hen."

"Once is an accident, Susan. But twice—"

"Is also an accident," she said firmly. "And very bad luck on my part. What else could it be?"

He was silent, his face expressionless. But underneath she sensed a cold anger directed not at her, but elsewhere. At the driver of the car, she was sure.

"Nothing else but coincidence," she lied in answer to her own question. "Horrible coincidence. I suppose I wasn't paying attention to traffic. The sun must be frying my brains."

"I'm beginning to think you need a keeper, *chère*." He traced her cheek with his forefinger. "I'll get you some aspirin. You're going to feel very bruised later."

"I feel it now," she admitted. Her muscles were protesting the least movement.

When he left the room, she let out her breath. He was suspicious, but he had accepted her explanation for the moment. She wanted desperately to accept her explanation, too, but she knew better. Nobody was nearly run over twice in two days without a reason.

And she had given someone a reason.

She closed her eyes, the mental anguish far beyond any physical pain. He must have seen her outside his house. He must know more than she'd imagined in her worst nightmares. Unconsciously she hadn't even allowed herself to think of it. She was paying for that now.

But she hadn't paid all the way. Not yet. That was to her advantage. Ross was brilliant and Ross was ruthless. He would try something else.

She instantly thought of Remy. He was angry and upset with a careless driver—but wondering. She should have kept away from him, as all her instincts had insisted she do. But she hadn't. Instead, she had fallen in love with him. Now she was tumbling him into a hornet's nest of danger. And then there was her grandmother. They were both so dear to her, and they were innocents who couldn't be exposed to this. She had to protect them.

Her stomach gave a sickening lurch at the thought.

Remy listened to the tenth unanswered ring,

then slammed down the receiver of his motel room telephone.

"Damn you, Ross Mitchelson," he swore. "Where the hell are you?"

He had left Susan only at her insistence and only to change out of his still-damp denim shorts. Still, he hadn't protested too much. He had wanted to call Ross to give him this latest news. He didn't care that he was doing it openly from his motel room. But four attempts had brought no answer.

He had wanted to get a feel for Ross's voice, he thought murderously, to listen to what the man *wasn't* saying.

"And then get Susan the hell undercover," he muttered through clenched teeth.

Every instinct had screamed at him when that car had been bearing down on Susan. And every damn one of them had been saying, "Ross." He still didn't have the gameboard, but Ross had to be a major player.

He would have to get the answers out of Susan, Remy thought, and he'd better get back to her right away.

He had just pulled on slacks and a shirt when the telephone rang. He snatched it up.

"Yes?"

"Remy, it's Lettice Kitteridge. I'm really worried about Susan. She wouldn't talk to me, she wouldn't listen to reason—"

His muscles tightened at the distress in the woman's voice. "What's the matter? Is she hurting worse?"

"No. I don't know. She was lucid when she went upstairs to lie down. But she came back down with a packed bag—"

"Packed!" Remy exclaimed, anxiety pumping through his veins. "Packed for what? The hospital?"

"No. She thanked me for a wonderful time, gave me a back-breaking hug, and said she had to leave. She had even called a taxi. Remy, you better go find her."

"What are you talking about, dammit!" he shouted.

"I'm not deaf!" Lettice shouted back. "I said Susan left! She packed a bag and took a taxi—"

"Why the hell didn't you stop her!"

"There was no time to stop her! She was gone while I was still gaping. Remy, you have to find her. She's sick, and she looks scared—"

"Okay." Susan was running. Definitely running, and he had no idea where. He remembered another taxi ride and hope welled up inside him. "I'll get her, Lettice."

He hung up the phone, grabbed his car keys, and ran out the door. He drove to the train station carefully, knowing if he didn't, the results could be disastrous. But the moment he parked the car, his fear was riding him to new heights. He had banked on the train station, but now he wondered if she had gone to the small airport to try to hire a plane.

He spotted her the instant he was inside the station. She was buying her ticket, and he strode over to her without a second thought. He had nearly reached her when she looked up. He took her arm before she could do anything more than stare.

"You can't go far enough, *chère,* that I won't ever find you."

Nine

Susan stared at him, fear crashing through her.

"How—" she began in a threadbare whisper, "how did you find me?"

"Lettice sent me after you," he snapped. She had never seen him look so angry before. His features could have been carved from marble, for all the cold expression in them. "Why didn't you come to me, Susan?"

"Here's your ticket, miss," the clerk said, pushing a stub through the slot of his wire cage.

She picked it up with shaking fingers. She had thought the spur-of-the-moment plan to get away would succeed because it *was* spur of the moment. She had checked behind her taxi all the way to the station, and she was positive no one had followed. She had furtively watched the people inside the station, and no one had paid attention to her or looked suspicious. She had thought herself safely away with only a major fight from her grandmother. But if Remy had found her so easily, so would others. Her stomach rolled at the horrible thought.

"I have to go," she forced herself to say. Her voice was calm and firm. "I can't stay. And it's not up for discussion—"

"Another of the same," Remy said to the clerk, shoving several bills through the slot.

"Remy, what are you doing?"

He didn't answer until his train ticket was in his hand. "Let's go."

"But—"

She had no time to protest as he hustled her through the station to the track platforms. She was numb with shock, conscious only of his strong fingers gripping her elbow, guiding her through the people. Their train was on the track already, its engine throbbing heavily. It was a mid-evening commuter and due to leave in a few minutes. Passengers were still filing onto it.

"Take the last car," Remy said, steering her to its door.

She stopped dead. "Remy, you're not going with me. I . . . it's dangerous to be with me."

"We'll argue the point on the train," he said, then grabbed her around the waist and hoisted her onto the car's steps.

She opened her mouth to protest.

"You're the one who's in a hurry," he reminded her.

She immediately closed her mouth and climbed into the car's interior. Remy was right behind her. The car was packed, nearly standing room only. Half the passengers were little old lady gamblers going home with their winnings, and the other half were casino employees exhausted from dealing all day with little old lady gamblers.

Remy directed her to the front of the car, where there were still several empty seats.

"Here," he said, and they sat down together on a small bench that faced the back of the train. It was also on the far side from the platform, and she could see out easily, but it would be difficult for anyone to see her. She was very aware of Remy's body, warm and comforting next to hers—and she was scared out of her wits that he was with her.

"Remy—"

"Wait until we're moving."

"No. That will be too late." She kept her voice low. She had to convince him to leave her. If he didn't . . . She cared for him too much to allow that to happen. Clearly Ross knew a lot more than she had thought. In the space of a few short days he had engineered two "accidents." She still didn't have anyone to go to, but she knew she had to go somewhere to stay safe. "I don't know how you found me, but get off this damn train now!"

"I bought a ticket, *chère*."

"I don't care. I don't want you here."

"You've got me here. Besides, you're in no condition to be going anywhere alone after that little two-step we did with that car. So wherever you go, I go."

She glared at him as he twisted in the seat to look out the window. Whatever her bruises were, they were far outweighed by her fear. The last time she had taken a train, it had been to solve her problems. This time it was to run. Fear surfaced again, and she swallowed back tears. It was hopeless, she thought. The driver of that car would find her. And Remy. She had a protector she didn't want . . . and yet wanted desperately.

"You don't understand," she said. "I'm in trouble."

"That wasn't hard to figure out." He gave her a quick smile. "Relax, *chère*. We'll get you out of it."

"But you don't know what it is."

"I have great faith."

She turned and gazed out the window, frustrated and frightened. Then she realized she hadn't been watching for people watching for her. She glanced around with as much curious innocence as she could muster. She was pretty sure all but two of the car's occupants had gotten on before them. Fortunately nobody looked the least bit interested in her. Still . . .

The conductor called a last "all aboard," then the train jolted forward. Gaining speed, it quickly pulled out of the station. They were on their way.

Remy turned to her. "Okay, so where *are* we going?"

"Damn you," she said, smiling and swiping at a tear at the same time. "What the hell do you think you're doing?"

"We did this lesson already. I am going with you. Lesson number two is: where are we going?"

She took a shaking breath. "Away. I don't know and I don't care."

"Why don't you tell me about it," he suggested gently.

She knew she shouldn't. Events had made it dangerous enough for her to know what she did. But he was so calm and so self-assured. Maybe if she told him, she could then persuade him to get help. She had no idea what kind, but it didn't matter. He would be away from her and safe.

She took another deep breath. "Those two near accidents were no accidents. I work for the government, Remy. Very few people know that. Remember the friend I told you about the day we went to see Sister Stephen?"

He frowned. "The friend in trouble?"

"Yes." Keeping her voice low, she went on. "My husband was with the State Department. He was killed in an automobile accident three years ago, and in the aftermath it was discovered that he'd been selling secrets to a foreign government. For a while I was under suspicion. A man named Ross Mitchelson was the head investigator, and he . . . well, he didn't believe it and he managed to prove my innocence. I was in shock, and he sort of took me under his wing. Less than a year later I went to work for him as a government courier."

Remy only raised his eyebrows.

She swallowed. "A few weeks ago I saw him take money from a senator's aide—"

"What!" Remy's jaw literally dropped open with astonishment.

Susan stared at him, bewildered by his reaction. "It was a lot of money in a briefcase. They were checking it, and I could see the stacks from where I was standing. He didn't see me that time. I'm sure of it. But I was so shocked . . . and scared. I knew that aide was considered a possible security risk because of suspected contacts with a certain unfriendly government. I just left everything and came to my grandmother's. Ross must have known something was wrong."

"You said he didn't see you 'that time,'" Remy prompted her.

"Yes. He was that 'business' I had to take care of several days ago. He had been my friend, and I wanted to get everything out so I could go on with my life. I owed him something, and I thought maybe if I talked to him, I could persuade him to stop or confess or . . . I don't know. When I arrived at his house, I realized how stupid I was, and I got right back in the cab."

"Right back? Didn't you see him or talk to him?"

She shook her head. "I . . . couldn't go in."

He hugged her, all the while grinning like a kid with a new toy.

"Remy, this is not good news!" she said nervously. "I think he must have seen me and figured something out. Now I need help. I have to find someone to tell this to, someone who can do something about it." Her lower lip trembled, and she bit it hard to regain her composure. Out of the corner of her eye she continually watched people for anything out of the ordinary, any sign of interest in her. There were none, but that didn't make her feel better. Unburdening herself on Remy did, however. He had taken her hand after the first few sentences and held it tightly, giving her strength. She felt wanted and cared for and hopeful again, not hopeless.

Finally she said, "I think Ross is involved in something far worse than bribes."

"I think you're right." He was silent for a long moment. "I wish you had told me this before."

"To what purpose?" she asked in disbelief. "What could I have said? That I was a spy who knew too much? You would have thought I was crazy. I'm trained not to say things, Remy. And I couldn't tell you this last part. I didn't even realize it all until today."

"That's a point."

"Now, will you please go away from me?" she asked, her voice breaking. "You're not involved in any of this, and it's not safe to be with me—"

"I thought that the first time I looked at you, *chère*." He put his arm around her, pulling her against him. His shirt caressed her cheek, and she inhaled his scent. It was an aphrodisiac.

"Now you know the real truth," she said.

"Finally."

She gazed up at him and forced out the rest of the words. "And now you'll go."

He kissed her gently, their lips meeting and clinging for a long moment. He lifted his head. "Not a chance."

Susan gasped back a sob of despair. "Remy, please!"

"You need help."

"Go and get it for me!"

"I intend to, believe me."

His words were sincere, but his attention was drawn to the window. Outside were only trees and deepening gloom. It had been that way almost from the moment they left Atlantic City. "We're deep in southern New Jersey," he said. "I think. All I've seen for a while now are trees."

"We're in the Pine Barrens," Susan said, dredging up tidbits of local geography from previous visits to her grandmother. "It covers the interior of this end of the state. It's a wilderness, really. Why?"

"Just needed to know where we are." He looked at his ticket and asked, "Are any of these stops in this Pine Barrens, do you know?"

She glanced at the ticket. None of the town names were familiar. "I'm not sure."

"We should get off where we can get you help," he said. "A smallish town, but not too small would be best."

"But I was going to Philadelphia."

He squeezed her hand. "You need rest, and the sooner the better. Besides, whoever is out there must know you'll head for the nearest city. They'll probably be there before you will. This is a cattle car making every stop."

"And that driver will be zooming along the expressway." She moaned, wondering frantically what to do.

"That's what they'll expect." He patted her arm. "Let's surprise them."

He was the one with the point this time, she thought, straightening. "I could keep my head start. If I can figure out where I'm going."

"That's lesson three."

She chuckled, almost relaxing. She was scared and tired and confused. And very grateful for Remy's calm presence. She never loved him more than now for insisting on staying. And she was never more furious with anyone. She hated to think of what he was getting into. She would have to get him out of it before he got in further, she decided. She wasn't able to stop him now, but when she acquired more private transportation . . .

She tucked her head into his shoulder, her mouth tightening. He wouldn't like what she was planning, but it was for his own good.

A short time later the Pine Barrens slowly gave way to more and more stretches of lights.

"Towns," Remy said, peering out the window. "Good sized ones too. We get off at the next stop, *chère*."

She turned his hand and glanced at his ticket. "Atco."

He frowned. "I beg your pardon?"

"That's the name of the stop. Atco."

"Okay." He sounded dubious.

Minutes later the train slowed, clearly coming into a station. People left their seats to stand by the doors. She started to get up, but he held her down.

"Wait until the last moment," he whispered in her ear. "After everyone else."

The doors opened, people went out. Others came in.

"Now."

They were up as one and moving so briskly for the doors, it was almost a run.

The doors were automatic and nearly shut in their faces. Remy literally banged them open again. They were through and out. He spun around and stared at the already-moving train. "Good. Nobody else almost 'missed' their stop like us."

Susan looked around at the tiny deserted station. The other people who had gotten off were already walking down the steps to the small parking lot. There were no waiting taxis, as there would be at a city station. In fact, the road passing the station had little traffic. There might be more lights, but there was no town she could see. Worse, there was no transportation. How, she wondered in dismay, were they going to get anywhere?

"Ah, Atco. You're my kind of town," Remy said, putting his arm around her and pointing to their left.

Susan looked, saw nothing, then looked up. The words NIGHT'S REST were boldly lit on a sixty-foot sign, announcing a chain motel was hidden behind the dense shrubbery.

She grinned.

Twenty minutes later they were ensconced in a small, clean room with one table, one bureau, two upholstered chairs, a nightstand, a TV, and a double bed. Susan sat down in one of the chairs. Her brain was numb and her body was aching with fatigue. Her throat was tight with unshed tears.

She wouldn't cry, she thought dimly. Kitteridges don't cry.

"Are you going to cry?" Remy asked after he was through inspecting the room.

"I'm trying not to." She forced herself to smile. Once she was rested, she would talk him into finding someplace to rent a car. And then she'd leave him at the first opportune moment. He wouldn't like it, but that was the only way she could assure his safety. "Unfortunately I'm not very well trained for when things go wrong in my line of work."

He knelt down in front of her and brushed the hair back from her face. "You're doing just great."

"No, I'm not." She wrapped her arms around his neck and burst into tears. "See?"

Remy held her close, horrified to see her cry like that. She was safe and hidden. Didn't she realize that? Then he realized that was exactly why she was crying. She was finally allowing herself the privilege.

He tightened his embrace, knowing now how much she had held back. Incredible, he thought, stroking her hair. She was incredible to come through what she had with such control.

All the game pieces had fallen into place with a snap when she had told him about Ross. The conflict between the information he was receiving about Susan and what he had seen finally made sense. Too much sense. A part of him exalted over being right all along. His instincts had been working beyond capacity this time. With the way Ross had twisted enough of the truth through the deceptions, it was no wonder he couldn't quite sort everything out.

Then anger shot through him, cold and piercing. He remembered the job he had been on before being sent to watch Susan. He had been tracing the rumor of a highly placed turncoat, and his last bit of information had made a connection to a senator's aide as a conduit. Ross was the turncoat. The realization was shocking. He knew exactly how Susan felt. Ross had befriended him too.

And Ross had a good reason to send him to watch Susan. Ross had known Remy was on his trail, and he'd somehow known Susan had seen a payoff from the other side. He had wanted to keep his "problems" in the same place while he figured out how to eliminate the damage without causing more. Their friend Ross was methodical and ruthless.

He had to get Susan to someone who could help them. The question was who. He worked too far on the outside to know anyone or the alliances within the government. And Remy had no idea who else might be involved with Ross. They'd have to stay undercover until he could find out.

Susan sagged against him, her crying jag done. It had been brief and bitter, and he hated Ross all the more for what he had done to her. He had recruited her when she had been most vulnerable, and he'd done it in the name of friendship. Remy wondered now just how much Susan had been used in her job as courier. More, he suspected, than anyone would ever know.

He would have to tell her about himself now, he realized. He hadn't on the train because they had been too busy dealing with her end of it. It hadn't been the time to throw her another curve. He had a feeling she wouldn't like *his* end of it anyhow. Not at all.

He decided he'd better get everything out in the open. He had no doubt she would understand his slight deception when he finished his explanation, especially when he told her how Ross had been feeding him conflicting information. He also realized he'd better get in a more comfortable position before he did. His knees were protesting loudly.

He rose to his feet, bringing Susan with him, and she melted against him. He wiped away the last tears with a tenderness that overwhelmed him. Another set of puzzle pieces fell into place.

"I love you, *chère.*"

She made a tiny noise in the back of her throat, and he stiffened. He was more frightened of a rejection from her than of anything Ross might be cooking up for them.

She raised her head. Her face was tear-streaked. "Remy, no."

His instincts told him the protest was for him, not a reflection of what she felt about him. And he always listened to his instincts. "Yes, Susan."

He lowered his head and took her lips in an all-encompassing kiss. She resisted for one awful moment . . . then wound her arms around his neck. Her mouth opened beneath his with a power that left him gasping for air. Her tongue made gentle demands on his own, demands he was overjoyed to answer. He wanted her to feel everything he felt. Nothing was more important than that.

She kissed him again and again. It was as if she couldn't get enough, and as if she were afraid she would. He knew she was frightened and unsure of everything right then. He himself was unsure of a lot of things, too, but he was damn sure of her.

Comfort and love eventually gave way to desire. Their mouths fueled the change. His hands stopped rubbing her back and began to stroke. Slowly he touched her, mesmerized by the warmth of her skin through her light knit top. He slipped his fingers underneath it, finding the soft flesh of her waist. It was unbelievable that he could have lost her just hours earlier to a car.

Some shred of common sense surfaced in his mind. She must be still hurting from the accident, he thought. And he was supposed to be telling her his role in her crisis.

"Susan, we should talk," he said, breaking off the kiss.

She pulled his head back down and whispered against his lips. "I love you and I need you. There may never be another time."

"But the car today . . . You were hurt . . ." He tried to think, but her lips were clinging to his, her fingers traveling along his ribs in slow, sensual patterns.

"Remy, please."

He was lost. He carried her the few steps to the bed and laid her down. She pulled him with her, their mouths meeting in a fire that engulfed them. Love and fear and want wrapped themselves around his brain until he couldn't think of anything else but them together like this. He had held his patience beyond endurance for so long. There would never be a right time, he knew. There would only be this time.

He tasted her with a keenness born of need, the

sweetness of her rocking the very core of him. He traced her cheek, her neck, her shoulder, her skin like silk under his mouth. Clinging to him, she whispered his name, nearly driving him insane. He sat up long enough to pull off her top and his shirt, then slipped away her bra to reveal her breasts. The nipples were already tight. She offered herself to him, her hands stroking his chest, her palms delicate and sensual against his skin.

He lowered his head and took her into his mouth. She moaned and writhed beneath him, her fingers digging into his shoulders. He drank her in as his hand traced the slope of her other breast. Her nails nearly scored his flesh when he rubbed his thumb across the nipple. She was wild under his touch, and satisfaction ran through him.

She had only to touch him, too, and he was driven to the brink himself. Her hands were setting fires all over his body with their tender demands. He had known it would be this way between them. He had sensed it from the first. It was a miracle he had held back with her this long.

She pulled his head up for her kiss. Their mouths fused in a heat that couldn't be stopped. The need to feel her, all of her, against him, at one with him, consumed him. The rest of their clothes were stripped away in a flurry of hasty hands.

Remy traced the curve of her waist and hips in wondrous awe. Her body glowed like antique satin in the lamplight. Her thighs were soft, meant to cradle a man's hardness with feminine power and love. Her tender flesh . . . He couldn't breathe, couldn't think beyond her. Every twist, every turn in his embrace drove him more out of control. She was mysterious, all fire under an amused, secretive smile. It was as if she had been made for him, only him. She was an obsession that would last a lifetime.

Susan ran her hands lovingly across his shoulders, feeling the muscles and the strength of this man. It was sweet and bitter to be with him like this, to know that it might only be this time. But she had waited too long for Remy. Her fingers delighted in following the whorls of hair on his chest. His body was marble, smooth and hard, and she took pleasure in him. Their thighs moved together until one of hers was captured between his. The sensation of smooth pressed to rough made her moan, and she gave herself up to the touch of his hands. They were gifted, finding by instinct places that drove her beyond reason. His mouth left burning kisses across her breasts, branding her flesh as his.

"I love you, Remy," she whispered.

She pulled at him, urging him forward until he found the moistness of her. He groaned her name and tilted her hips, and she took him inside her. Both of them gasped at the tender shock of flesh within flesh. The rightness of it nearly broke her, and she buried her face in his shoulder.

"I've wanted you for so long, *chère*," he murmured, holding her tightly.

She kissed him in answer, and they moved together. Quickly they found the unique rhythm of man and woman. Everything was shed away except this culmination of love. With every thrust, each demanded more from the other. And with every thrust, each gave to the other. Remy was driving her higher and higher with him in a force so gentle she never wanted it to stop. But the spinning mist was coming at her, even as she heard him cry out her name. It enveloped her, swirling her into its vortex, Remy the only reality . . . until they were both wrapped together in the silken darkness that followed.

Awareness surfaced slowly. Susan tried to push it away, but it refused. She took a deep breath, inhaling the scents of her and Remy mingled. She smiled sadly, her hands stroking his cool skin in the aftermath of love. She had deceived him, she thought. Even now she had been selfish and deceptive in her love for him. How could she go through with her plan to leave him the moment she had a car? Just to dump him when his guard was down, even if it were for his own safety. She couldn't do that. She would have to persuade him, an *honest* persuasion, to stay behind.

"I love you," he murmured, opening his eyes.

His expression, his contented smile, told her how much he meant the words. She suppressed the urge to cry and kissed him instead.

"Remy, we need to talk."

He drew in a deep breath and exhaled. "I know."

"You cannot go with me," she said, running her hands along his back. He moved, and to still his coming protest she added, "I'm sorry, but I've thought about this. It's too dangerous for you to be with me even now. You can't go with me—"

"Yes, I can."

"Remy—"

He kissed her. After he lifted his head, he touched her lips with his finger, then said, "I'm not an innocent. I work for the Company—"

"What!" She struggled to sit up, but he held her tightly.

"You're not going to like it, but you'll understand when you hear me out."

She stilled, her stomach churning with anger and shock.

Remy continued. "I couldn't tell you before. I work for a special branch, a watchdog force that investigates suspected turned agents among other trouble-shooting duties. Ross pulled me off another case and sent me to watch you. He told me you were about to sell some information . . ."

It was a nightmare, Susan thought, listening numbly.

"After I saw you, saw the sadness in you, *chère*, it didn't take me long to realize you were in trouble, that someone had set you up. Now we know it was Ross."

"You've been spying on me," she finally whispered in a choked voice.

"Yes. Susan, be thankful I have, that it was me. I knew something was wrong almost from the beginning. I've been watching *over* you for a long time now, while I've been trying to figure out what's really going on. Today, though, when you told me your side, everything fell into place. My other case was following a rumor of a highly placed turned agent with some connection to a senator's aide. *Ross* is the highly placed turned agent—"

"Did you have me bugged?" she asked coldly.

He stared at her, then snorted and smiled wryly. "No. Of course not."

He began to stroke her arm. She stiffened and pulled away.

"You promised to listen—"

"No, I didn't." She pushed his arms away as he tried to hold her. Pain knifed through her, almost unbearable in its intensity. She felt so used and so foolish. It hurt to know how she had come to trust him implicitly, how she had refused to be . . . dirty and check up on him. He was as phony as her husband had ever been—more—and she had been completely deceived. She began to pull on her clothes, ashamed now and vulnerable in her intimacy. She had made love with him, *made love*, and never sensed just how far wrong she was about him. He had hurt her more than anyone ever had before.

He sat up. "*Chère*, please just listen."

"I did." She flung away his hands. "All this time, Remy, you let me believe you were an innocent French-Canadian businessman on vacation. But you're no businessman, are you?"

He winced. "Well, I'm not exactly French-Canadian either."

Her jaw dropped at this new shock.

He brightened. "But it wasn't really a lie. My ancestors were Acadian. I'm Cajun, from Louisiana."

"Cajun!" She glared at him. His expression was charmingly innocent, and she hated him for it. "I didn't even get that right, did I?" she said bitterly.

"Now, *chère*, it's not that bad," he began.

She leapt off the bed. "You lie to me, you play games with me, and it's not that bad? Not five minutes ago you said you loved me—"

"And I meant it!" He tried to take her hand.

She stepped back. "I don't believe you."

"Susan!"

"I don't believe you." She glanced around the room. "You led me right to this place, right inside and made love to me. Is the room bugged? Is this where Ross walks in and says, 'How nice. Finish her'? And what's your line? 'Gee, *chère*, sorry, but love doesn't conquer all'?"

His look was deadly. Fear clawed at her, but she refused to show it.

Instead of attacking her, he did the most mundane of things. He pulled on his briefs. "I didn't lead you anywhere. If you'll remember, you were the one sneaking out of town. I watched over you. I kept faith, Susan, even after your little visit to Ross. What I thought—" He waved a hand, interrupting himself. "He set me up as much as he did you. He knew what I was uncovering. He knew I would get too close. We've been lucky so far, that he hasn't been successful. I can understand your anger, but I'm not a bastard. It's both of us he wants to stop."

"I'm leaving," she said, picking up her purse.

"To go where?" he asked smugly. "Ross's maniac car driver is out there looking for you. And there will be others. We have to go into hiding—"

"Not with you."

"Susan, don't be foolish."

"I already have been." Fury fueled her. "You seduced me into accepting you. You lied to me every second we were together. You made love to me with a lie. I'll never forgive you for that."

"Fine!" he snapped, waving his arm. "But use your head. You and I have to get to someone who will believe us and who is powerful enough to take on Ross. We have a better chance of doing that if we're together. Just think about that for one damn minute."

She knew he was right, and she hated him for that too. She had been a low-level courier who knew nobody beyond Ross. She knew a good number of the political power brokers through her family and from the party circuit. But she didn't know who stood where on the subject of Ross. If she made one mistake now, approached the wrong person, she'd never approach another. That was sure. But it was clear Remy had been in the secrets business for a long time. She cursed under her breath at the thought. It would hurt so much to be around him.

"You know I'm right, don't you," he said, no question in his tone. "You know Ross is ruthless. You know he'll do anything to keep you silent. And me. Use any method to bring us out in the open . . ."

His voice trailed away as he stared at her.

She stared back, the same horrible realization dawning.

"Lettice!"

"Ross will use her for a hostage," Remy exclaimed, "to bring us out."

"I know." Scared for her grandmother, Susan leapt for the telephone. Remy grabbed it out of her hands.

"Remy!"

"We don't know about the phones there. We'll go back and get her."

"That will waste time!"

"Probably, but it can't be helped." He was so calm, she wanted to smack him into reality. "We can't call. And we can't have her come to us. She might be followed. And if someone is with her, then she won't come at all. So we go back for her."

"I'll find the train schedule."

"No trains."

"And how do you propose we get there?" Susan

asked caustically, sniffling back fearful tears. "With our good looks?"

He grinned. "It depends on the finances, *chère*. Find the telephone book, find the nearest car rental place, a local one, find a taxi to get us there, and find it now. It will take them a while to trace a rental car."

She glared at him. "And what will you be doing while I'm doing all the work?"

He snapped the waistband of his briefs. "Getting dressed. And thinking. I'm the professional of this outfit, remember?"

She grimaced. "Then we're in worse trouble than I thought."

She began searching drawers for the telephone book.

Ten

The car was deadly silent.

It was after midnight when they drove over the Longport bridge onto the barrier island that housed Atlantic City and its environs. They were coming in by the back end of town in the hope that this small bridge wouldn't be watched as the expressway would. Susan hadn't spoken a word since they had made the last-minute rental from a closing agency. She hadn't accepted the truth with quite the understanding Remy had been hoping for.

He knew she had every right to be angry, but he was angry with her. How could she think he would be so cold as to make love to her and then . . . Hadn't she learned anything about him over the past weeks? Didn't she know what *he* had gone through to keep his belief in her? Granted, she had been through a lot and didn't know who to trust. But it hurt to know she didn't trust him.

He glanced over at her. Her hair hid her face, but he had no doubt its expression would freeze

Lake Ponchartrain with one glance. Their love-making had been incredible. He could still taste her, still feel her moving with him in such passion . . . and love. Dammit, he thought. He loved her, he had held on through the worst, and she refused to understand.

He glanced at her again, and his anger gave way to sympathy. She was scared and angry herself. She'd come around, he decided optimistically. She would realize that if he had had any choice in the matter, he would have made a confession ages before. He'd been telling himself that for the last fifty miles. Unfortunately the notion kept surfacing that he'd done the unforgivable with her. He couldn't shake the thought that it hadn't been his logic, but her own, that persuaded her to stay with him.

"*Chère*, your grandmother will be fine," he said, attempting conversation.

Silence.

"They'll be too busy trying to find us to think of her yet. We're in time, I'm sure."

Silence.

"They'd probably throw her back anyway," he muttered, curling his fingers around the steering wheel. Okay, so it was taking her a little bit longer to forgive him than he'd thought.

Ten minutes later they had the car parked on the street behind the Kitteridge house and were slipping through the yards. The house was dark except for a light in the TV room. Through the curtains on the veranda doors, they could see Lettice moving about. Remy motioned for Susan to stay in the shadow of the fir trees. Every one of his senses was attuned for the least odd rustle on the property. When he was finally assured no one else was hiding furtively in the bushes beside them, he touched her arm and they moved toward the house.

He breathed a huge sigh of relief when they reached the veranda safely. Sweat trickled down his cheek. Susan's face looked ghostly white as she peered inside the doors.

Remy patted her arm, then boldly opened the doors.

Lettice spun around, her astonished expression quickly turning to relief.

"It's about damn time!"

Remy immediately put his finger to his lips, while Susan, with great presence of mind, turned up the TV set's volume.

"Get cash and a jacket," Remy said in a low voice. "We're going now."

Lettice gaped at them. "Wha—"

"Do it," Susan said, taking her grandmother's arm. "Remy and I are in trouble."

Her grandmother's eyebrows shot up. "Do you have to get married?"

"I wish," Remy muttered, impatient with Lettice's delay. They had to get out now. "Susan—"

"I know where they are." She let go of her grandmother's arm and swept out of the room. Remy glanced after her, amazed that she had known what he wanted before he said it.

"I want to know what this is all about," Lettice said. "You two are acting like spies."

"We are," Remy said. "And keep your voice down."

Lettice's eyes grew round as her mouth opened and closed. She was finally and completely astonished into silence.

Susan was back in the room with her grandmother's jacket and purse before Remy had begun to worry about her. She took her grandmother's hand and squeezed it reassuringly. This time Lettice made no protest as they walked out onto the veranda. Susan closed the doors behind them. They were through the backyard and in the car, Remy speeding off, before another minute had passed. He had deliberately picked a car that was the same style as five others at the agency, and he'd muddied the license plate, so it was unreadable in the dark. Susan watched behind them without being told as he swerved through the deserted streets.

"No one's following," she said, finally turning back around.

He grinned. She *was* incredible.

"Now, will somebody tell me just what is going on?" Lettice demanded in a voice that brooked no argument. It was clear she'd sat quietly in the backseat long enough.

"You start," Remy said to Susan.

"I intended to," she replied frostily.

Remy gritted his teeth. So much for the rapport.

Susan told her grandmother the same story she had told him. She also explained why they had come back for Lettice and just how dangerous they thought Ross could be. Her voice held only a trace of anxiety in the telling. Remy admired her for her control and loved her for her bravery. He couldn't think of a single other person he'd want at his back in a time like this.

"And you were quite right about *our* Remy, Grandmother," Susan went on. "He wasn't the man *I* thought he was. He's no businessman from Canada. He's a very special agent for the Company. And he's been spying on us all this time, infiltrating our confidence and our emotions to get information *any* way he could—"

"Now, just a damn minute!" Remy exclaimed.

Susan rounded on him. "No, you wait just a damn minute! You were lying the entire time to me and to my grandmother." She turned back to Lettice. "He lied about everything. He thought I was selling government secrets and he was sent to spy on me. Me! As if I would ever do such a thing. My father was an ambassador, for goodness' sake!"

"I was doing my job, dammit!" he snapped. "And when I saw everything was all wrong from what I'd been told, I had to get closer to find the truth. And to watch over you. Why can't you understand that?"

"Because you did it too well, Remy." Her voice caught. "Because you were too thorough . . . and too good . . . and you never once, knowing that I was in trouble, told me who you really were."

The silence was so tense, Remy thought the car would burst from the pressure. He refused to answer. He'd explained himself more than once already. If she couldn't understand, then he damn well wasn't wasting any more breath.

"That explains a lot," Lettice finally said, "although I'm still thoroughly confused. You're really a courier, Susan?"

"Yes."

"And you, Remy, are an honest-to-goodness James Bond?"

He chuckled. "Hardly James Bond."

"You mean there's no Aston-Martin with all the gadgets?"

Remy gave her the bad news. "I don't even have a gun."

Lettice choked. "No gun! We have all these people after us and you don't even have a gun! What kind of spy are you anyway?"

"He's more like the bad guys," Susan said. "At least he has their nasty voyeur practices."

Forgiveness looked about as close as Jupiter, Remy decided. But he held his temper and watched the road behind them. It remained clear.

"Well," Lettice said, patting him on the back, "I'm very glad to know you're not some sleazy fortune hunter."

He grinned, feeling as if he'd received a stamp of approval.

"So where are we going now, Susan?"

"Ask the 'professional' of the group, Grandmother," Susan suggested sweetly.

Remy glared at her, then said, "We're going into hiding until we can contact somebody who has the clout to expose this to the right people. It could take a while." A thought occurred to him, and he chuckled. "You know, Lettice, we're making the spy record books. It's not every day two spies take a grandmother into hiding with them."

"And you're not taking this one," Lettice said. "I can't go into hiding. I'm supposed to see my sister tomorrow."

"You can see her when everything is over," Remy said.

"In a pig's eye I will! She's expecting me and she'll be very upset. In fact, so will Mamie, my housekeeper. My sister can give her a message—"

"I'm sorry, Lettice, but we'll probably have a lot of people upset before this is over—"

"You stop this damn car right now!" Lettice snapped. "I am getting out."

"Grandmother, please." Susan reached over the

seat and took Lettice's hands. "We can't stay until tomorrow. We have to get as far away from here as possible—"

"Then I'll see her now. Remy, take us to the convent."

"At this time of night?" he exclaimed. "We can't wake the convent up, Lettice. We've got people after us. Every minute's delay means their getting closer to Susan and me—"

"You came all the way back for me, didn't you?" Lettice asked with great satisfaction. "For my protection. Now I will not go until I see my sister and let her know I'll be all right and she should watch herself. It's twenty minutes down the road, and we can spare the time for the detour. Now, you get this car moving toward Loveladies, Remy, or I will never forgive you."

"Remy, you better take her." Susan gazed at him, looking almost resigned. "Believe me, it will be a whole lot easier if you do."

He gripped the wheel in a stranglehold. He was going to kill them both.

After they saw Lettice's sister.

"Now, was that visit worth it or not?"

Susan felt her lips curve in an unwanted smile at her grandmother's smug tone.

"Very," Remy agreed. "I forgive you."

Susan lost all amusement when he spoke, pain and anger filling her again. She stared out the car window. It was a few hours until dawn and they were finally speeding through the back roads of the Pine Barrens, officially on their way into hiding—wherever that was. Only the "professional" knew for sure.

She grimaced. The last thing she wanted to do was go anywhere with Remy. But she was trapped.

She watched his hands guide the car with a deft touch. Those same hands had guided her, skimming across her body with the knowledge of desire. Those same hands had brought her to the brink of pleasure, then sent her plunging over the edge. She could still feel him hard and strong against her, still feel the unique pleasure his mouth had created, still feel them moving together as one. Her blood surged up from deep inside her and coursed along her veins in a slow, pulsing rhythm, just as it had before. She couldn't think, almost couldn't breathe as her body was caught by the momentary sensations. They ebbed at last, leaving her shaken that she could feel their re-membered lovemaking so vividly. They had been one, she thought, closing her eyes. And then they had been shattered apart by the truth.

Now she knew what was "not right" about Remy. She had insisted on ignoring the signs and being completely honest with him. She had wanted his actions to speak for themselves. Well, they had spoken.

Part of her wanted to believe he hadn't been using her, that he could have done nothing more than he had. She forced the disturbing thought away. She had been stupid enough already when it came to Remy St. Jacques. She wouldn't com-pound it.

"I still can't get over it," Lettice said, interrupt-ing her granddaughter's unhappy musings. "I had never known about my sister and the war. She didn't quite lock herself away—at least not as I'd thought."

Susan smiled, gratefully remembering their detour. They had awakened the convent, Lettice demanding to see her sister and Remy cursing under his breath the entire time. Sister Stephen hadn't needed a second explanation of their trouble. In fact, she had become a gentle commander, giving orders and instructions to help them along their way. It turned out that Sister Stephen had been assigned to a convent in France during World War II, where she had helped many people get out of the country. One of them had been a downed American pilot, who was now an adviser to the President. Sister Stephen vowed "Neddy" was absolutely trustworthy and he owed her a favor. She would call and smooth the way for them. They didn't doubt her for a moment.

"Theodore Casper," Remy said. "Your sister performed a miracle, Lettice."

"Mmm. Now I have to perform one."

The hairs on Susan's neck rose, and a vague alarm went off inside her. Lettice's words sounded ominous, but she wasn't sure why. She was extremely grateful for her grandmother's presence just then, though. Lettice was once again providing a wonderful barrier between her and Remy.

"I have my own miracle performing to do," Remy said. "I have to get us all to Casper in one piece. Susan, how are you feeling?"

She stiffened.

"After the car accident, I mean," he added hastily.

Her face reddened in humiliation. If he had drawn a picture for Lettice, he couldn't have gotten the point across as well.

"I'm fine," she said in as cool a voice as possible.

"Too tired?"

"No!" she snapped, then calmed down. "No more tired than you or Grandmother."

"Good."

His voice was cold, and she snapped her teeth together. It was clear he thought she was just being snippy for no reason, when he was making their private business as clear as a bell to the *last* person in the world who should know it. Her grandmother would have a field day with this. But she was not going to correct him and make matters worse.

"Are we taking the turnpike down to Washington, or using the back roads?" she asked, determined to change the subject.

"We're not," he said. "With Washington being only four hours away, they'll bet we'll make a straight run—after they decide that we'll think they won't. We're going west and south instead."

Susan swallowed. "How long are we talking about here?"

"Long enough. Don't worry, Susan. I won't annoy you more than I have to." His velvety whiskey voice lent itself well to sarcasm.

"Thank you. I appreciate that," she muttered.

She would take great pleasure in walking away from him with her head high and her pride intact, she thought furiously.

If they ever got out of this alive.

The best that could be said about the motel was that it was cheap . . . and in Gettysburg, Pennsylvania.

"You cannot stay in here with us!" Susan said as she stomped into the room. The vehemence in her voice matched the look on her face.

Remy closed the door on the afternoon sun and

glared at her. "I can and I will. We stay together for all our protection."

"Well, I am grateful for your presence," Lettice said, testing one of the double beds with her hand and frowning.

Remy stared at Susan, scarcely hearing Lettice. Susan stared back. He wanted to tell her he hadn't purposefully chosen a motel from the same chain as the night before. It had been a long stretch from the last lodging they'd seen, and he'd been too tired to wait for the next. All of them needed rest, and as they were hundreds of miles west now of the Jersey shore, they finally could. It would be a longer trek to the south before he'd swing back around to Washington. He couldn't help it that this room was almost identical to the other one they'd shared, although she was probably blaming him for that too.

"What are you afraid of, Susan?" he asked, his fingers tightening around the paper bags he held.

"Don't flatter yourself." Her lips thinned into a straight, uncompromising line.

"I'm glad that's all settled, children," Lettice broke in. "Now what?"

"Now we rest and eat," Remy snapped. "We all need it."

He dropped one of the bags on the table by the window, then strode over to the far bed and flopped down on it in his own test.

"It's not cordon bleu," he said, adjusting the pillows against the headboard so he could recline comfortably. He opened his bag and pulled out a fast-food cheeseburger and a milk shake. "But it'll do."

Susan glared at him one last time, then unpacked the rest of their meal. She sat down in one of the two chairs and began to eat.

Lettice picked up her burger and examined it. Shrugging, she unwrapped it and took a bite. "Not bad. But I like Burger Heaven better."

For one unguarded moment Susan glanced at Remy in amusement. She instantly turned back to her meal, but he felt a minor victory.

Lettice brought her meal over to the far side of the other bed and sat down, clearly claiming it as her spot. Remy nearly choked on his sandwich at the unexpected action. For weeks Lettice had been trying to separate them, and now she was leaving her granddaughter no option but to take the near side of their bed—the side next to him. If he didn't know better, he'd swear he'd just acquired an ally in the cold war with Susan.

He glanced at her. Her eyes were wide and she sat as if frozen to the spot.

"So how did you ever get into the spy business, Remy?" Lettice asked.

"I was a rookie detective with the New Orleans police, when we uncovered a spy ring while on a drug case," he said, turning his attention to Lettice. "Ross liked the way I handled myself and recruited me for Internal."

"How did your family feel?" Lettice chuckled. "Did they know about your undercover work?"

"No." He shrugged. "My family thinks the CHT job is real. My father was a police captain, and he wasn't happy that I left the force for a salesman's job."

"Doesn't he know now?" Susan asked.

"No. He never did."

The old argument was still a raw spot, and he regretted that his father had never known the truth. Even knowing the truth herself, he thought, Susan would probably take the incident with his father as just another example of his "deceiving" nature. Would it always be his lot to lie to those he loved? Hell, everybody forgave Don Diego once they found out he was Zorro.

"Your father would have understood," Lettice said firmly. "After all, he was in a similar branch of work. And *I* understand you now. I was rude to you upon occasion, I believe. I hope you will forgive me."

"I already have." Remy smiled wryly, thinking it was the wrong Kitteridge woman who was doing the understanding.

"I think this is a mistake!" Susan exclaimed, bringing the conversation to an abrupt halt. She was on her feet and pacing the room. "Washington was only four hours away from Atlantic City. We could have made it—"

"Maybe, *chère*," he interrupted. "But those roads would have been heavily watched."

"So could the one you're planning to take!"

"I'm hoping Ross will get nervous when we don't show up today, and will concentrate his efforts on every little country road and hollow between Jersey and Washington." Remy grinned. "I wouldn't be surprised if he's searching the marinas too. It's probably occurred to him we could use the water. The car, which seems the easiest and fastest way, will now be thrown over in favor of other transportation. We leave this evening and drive through the night."

She whipped around, hugging herself tightly. He knew her fear was surfacing again. He desperately wanted to hold her and reassure her that they would somehow get through this together, but he knew she wouldn't accept him. If anything, she'd become even more upset. He set his jaw, knowing this was not the time. Once this was over, he would straighten this mess out with her and get things back to normal. He hoped.

"Susan, you need to rest," Lettice said, her voice all authority. "Now, come lie down and try to relax."

Susan hesitated for one moment, then strode over and lay down stiffly on the bed.

"I said relax!" Lettice exclaimed.

"I will, dammit," Susan snapped.

Remy let them argue. At least she wasn't snipping at him. Angry as she was at him, she still had lain down on his side of the bed. Lettice had a few more pointed comments about her granddaughter's relaxing, or lack of it, then she settled down.

He lay still as the room grew silent. At first he was able to ignore the space between the beds as he tried to relax and nap a little. Usually he could put everything out of his head and sleep at the first safe moment. But slowly his awareness of the slight distance between him and Susan occupied all of his thoughts.

He was too conscious of her soft breathing. Her legs shifted languidly, her thighs brushing together briefly. He could still feel those thighs, lush and silken, cradling him, urging him to her with passion. Her perfume drifted across the space, filling his senses with that unique scent only she possessed. It had haunted him for far too long for him not to know even the faintest breath of it.

He wanted to reach out and pull her to him, to kiss away the anger until she forgave him. The rest of the world could be damned for all he cared.

He turned his head to glance at her at the same moment that she shifted restlessly.

He found himself gazing into her wide-awake eyes.

He realized she hadn't meant to turn his way, that it must have been an unconscious action on her part. But she didn't move. She gazed back at him for a long moment. His breath caught at the hunger he read in her expression. She was so beautiful, he thought. He loved her. He wanted her so badly to be his again. Maybe . . .

He reached out across the three-foot space between them. Pain and anger crossed her features, shuttering the vulnerability that lay beneath. She rolled over, giving him her back.

Remy stared at the ceiling and drew in a deep breath to calm his frustrations. Much as he usually liked the view of the curving line of her body, he was in no mood for it at the moment.

Despite his attempt at control, his muscles were tense and his emotions were playing a fast-paced game of Ping-Pong between anger and patience. He remembered that Lee had lost the Civil War at Gettysburg.

His own battle had only begun.

The tiny, unbearable motel was hours behind them.

And it would take days to recover, Susan thought, staring out the window at the western edge of Maryland. She hadn't slept at all, and every aching, weary bone in her body was reminding her of that. Her grandmother, on the other hand, had fallen asleep like a newborn, awakened refreshed, and was now sound asleep again in the backseat. Susan vowed to disown her at the first opportunity.

The car seemed more cramped than ever. Susan kept herself as close to the passenger door as possible without being blatant about it. She might be furious, but she would not act like a teenager having a temper tantrum. Unfortunately she was aware of every shift, every movement Remy made as he drove the car. She decided maturity stank.

Her own brain felt foggy and numb, a state she was happy to have achieved under the circumstances. Now she only had to get her heart in similar order. The earlier conversation between Remy and Lettice ran through her mind again. The damn thing was like a broken record, she thought, repeating itself until her conscience wanted to secede from the rest of her. But she could not rid herself of the notion that Remy had done what was necessary for the most noble of reasons. He had had the honor to adhere to his commitments whatever the cost to himself. Worse, part of her was beginning to feel guilty for being angry—as if she were being unreasonable and in the wrong.

And then she had turned in that damnable bed at the same moment that he had turned to look at her. All her senses had been acutely attuned to him lying a short space from her. One look in his eyes, and she had ached to curl herself against his body . . . to feel again her softness yielding to his hardness. In that instant she had wanted so badly to be in his arms again.

Instead, Susan pushed back her hair and forced herself to think of the way he had lied. If only he had confessed before she had. Even if he had told her before they made love, she wouldn't be feeling so betrayed.

"What exits do we want to use, *chère*?" he asked. "I forget."

Her heart lifted at the endearment. She forced it back down and concentrated on the map. They were on a major interstate highway, Remy having decided the risk was nil to minimal. Besides, none of them knew the back roads at all and the map they'd gotten before leaving Gettysburg didn't show them. There were other cars on the highway, but traffic was thin with the late hour. From the wooded hills and fenced fields it was clear they were in rural surroundings.

"Winchester is the exit and we can pick up either seven or sixty-six," she said, keeping her voice polite. "Either leads into Arlington. We've got a while yet. Both are still several miles after we cross Harpers Ferry."

"Do you think we should go farther south?" he asked.

"I don't know," she said slowly. "We'd still have to come back at some point, and we'd still have to use one of the main roads to get into Washington. That whole area is a metroplex for D.C."

Remy glanced at her and smiled. "Once we get closer to the city, I think I can get us into Washington proper through some secondary roads."

"The trick is getting there, Remy."

"Zorro's never failed yet."

"Zorro?"

He chuckled. "Never mind, *chère*. Don't worry, we'll get there safe and sound."

"I bet Custer said that to his troops before Little Bighorn."

He grinned and patted her knee. She realized she was actually chatting with him and turned back in her seat, ready to keep him at bay.

A thump and a bang shuddered through the car like a jolt of lightning in a thunderstorm. The car lurched sickingly toward the shoulder guard-rail. Susan yelped and braced herself as Remy cursed and fought the wheel.

"What the hell does he think he's doing!" her grandmother screeched from the backseat.

Susan glanced around in time to see a car slamming into theirs again, trying to force them off the road. Sparks flew as the cars met with a shock of metal on metal. Fear shot through her at the thought of what might happen if the other car succeeded . . . and if they could miss the guard-rail at the speed they were traveling.

The cars broke apart and the other car came alongside them. Susan stared at it, but could see only a dark form behind the other car's wheel. She gasped as it swung wide to come at them again.

"Hang on to your seat belts, folks!" Remy yelled, and hit the brakes.

Eleven

Remy's timing was perfect.

The other car slid past them and into the guardrail, bounced off, spun around directly in front of them for a terrible second, then whirled back into the rail.

They sped past it. Susan stared in astonishment at the battered vehicle, the driver holding his head as he slumped over the wheel.

"Remy," she whispered. She reached for his hand automatically.

He let go of the wheel with one hand and gripped hers tightly, his fingers warm and comforting and alive. He glanced over at her. "Are you okay, *chère*?"

She was quaking inside with shock, and her brain was reeling with a jumble of emotions. "Yes, I'm okay. You?"

"Okay."

She smiled at him. He smiled back. His expression held reassurance—and something more. Something she wasn't ready to deal with yet. He gave her another quick smile, then turned back to the road.

She remembered there was another passenger in the car and jerked around in complete panic.

"Grandmother!"

"About time somebody remembered me," Lettice snapped, straightening in the seat. She patted her hair back into place. "I'm fine, except that man took ten years off my life that I can't afford to lose."

Susan sighed loudly in relief, then grinned.

"I should have known," Remy muttered.

"How do you think he got on to us?" she asked.

"I think he's been around from the beginning," Remy said, keeping his gaze on the highway. He had the car above the speed limit already. "We just didn't know it."

Anxiety crawled through her stomach. "What about others?"

"That's the question, isn't it?"

"Aren't we going to stop and take the driver into custody?" Lettice asked.

"No," Susan and Remy said at the same time.

"If we stop," Remy added, "we'll be there for hours with the cops doing accident procedurals. Then Ross will have us. Others will stop for the accident, although he didn't look badly hurt to me. Besides, we're not equipped to take prisoners. It's not a nice business, Lettice."

"And no guns either. So now what?"

Susan saw an exit sign looming in the distance. "So now we take the scenic route."

"Exactly," Remy said, satisfaction in his voice.

He let go of her hand to turn the wheel toward the exit ramp. Susan stared at her fingers, realizing that she had been holding his hand the entire time out of shock.

And out of love.

• • •

"Where are we?"

"Boonsboro," Susan answered, scrutinizing the map on her lap as she answered her grandmother.

"And just *where* is that?"

"Western Maryland. And stop being so crabby."

"I have a right to be crabby," Lettice snapped. "I'm old and I'm lost."

Remy mustered a chuckle. He was too tired to do anything else. They were all tired, but resting was out of the question at the moment. They had been riding almost aimlessly through the wilds of western Maryland, roundabout but keeping to a southeasterly direction during most of the night. The two-lane roads and small towns, while isolated, allowed him to watch the traffic very carefully. It was after dawn now and nobody was following them. Of that he was sure.

But they had been found once and they could be found again. He had an idea about that. It was one he didn't like at all.

Susan and her grandmother were beginning to bicker in earnest.

"Now, ladies," he said, attempting to head off a squabble. "We're just a little lost."

"No, we're not," Susan said brightly. "We're in Boonsboro."

"*Lost* in Boonsboro," Lettice added.

"But we're in Boonsboro," Susan said forcefully.

"And here to get a car," Remy added, not ready to referee another go-round. "Then we rest."

A short while later he parked the car on a downtown side street. Turning in the seat, he said to Lettice, "Now, you know what to do, right?"

She raised her brows in disdain. "I think I can manage to rent a car."

Susan glanced at him then took her grandmother's hand. "You'll be okay."

Lettice kissed her granddaughter's cheek, then got out of the car and walked up the street. He didn't say anything to Susan until her grandmother had turned the corner.

"I wish one of us could have done it," he said.

"You know it was too risky. Besides, she's eating this up. Are we changing cars for the reason I think we're changing cars? They managed to attach a remote 'finder' to this one somehow?"

He nodded, admiring her perception. "I think they did it when we went in to get Lettice. That was the only time we weren't with the car besides Gettysburg, and they couldn't have followed us just by sight all that way. I think our disappearance last night worried Ross, and when we showed up again we were 'allowed' to get your grandmother. He's probably wondering who else we might have talked to in that time."

"And they left us alone, staying far back, just watching where we were going . . . until we turned south again. That's when they rammed us."

He nodded. "They're most likely still a couple of miles back, tracking us—even in these mountains. I don't have time to look for the transmitter. I doubt I could find it anyway. Once we get the second car, we drive them both for a while, then ditch this one. Whoever it is will think we stopped for lunch."

She looked at him in hope. "Maybe we can get to Casper after all."

"Let's cross our fingers that he's the friendly ghost," Remy added.

The anger in her seemed to have disappeared, so he reached out and touched her cheek, hopeful and afraid of her reaction.

"Remy," she whispered.

The moment she said his name, he knew he was lost. He pulled her to him, and she was in his arms, real and pliant.

Their lips met in a kiss fierce with hunger and contrition and love. Her mouth fitted itself to his in a gentle demand. He tasted her, their tongues swirling together in mutual need. He slid his hands under her jacket to reassure himself that she was truly with him. He wanted to be alone with her, not in hiding but in passion, with the hours stretching endlessly before them. He vowed they would have such a time. And he would commit himself over and over to her. He didn't want to lose her again.

"When that car . . ." she began, her voice breaking when she was finally free to talk. "Remy, I realized how stupid I was."

"I know, I know," he murmured, kissing her cheeks, her forehead.

She started laughing. "Don't press your luck."

He realized what he said and chuckled against her soft skin. "That wasn't quite what I meant."

"No kidding." She held him tightly as she grew serious. "Remy, I understand why you couldn't tell me about yourself. After the shock wore off, I realized there probably wasn't anything else you could have done."

He brushed wayward strands of her hair away from her exotic features, marveling at her grace and his luck to have been forgiven. "I never meant to hurt you, *chère*. Never."

"I know. My husband—" She stopped. "I did feel stupid when I finally found out about him. This time I felt again as if my judgment were all wrong. Only it was worse. I had fallen in love with you."

He drew her to him again and inhaled the scent of her. It reached deep inside him, swirling around like a gentle cocoon, wrapping him up in her. He never wanted to be anywhere else.

"If we ever get out of this, marry me," he said.

She gasped and pulled back. For a long moment she searched his face, and he let her see everything.

"I—I don't know."

He stiffened, his arms dropping away. "What did you say?"

"I'm sorry, Remy," she said, looking unhappy. "I—I love you, but we also need to know each other better."

"I know I can trust you with my life. You know you can trust me with the same."

She touched his cheek. "I trust you with my heart."

"Then why the hesitation?" he demanded, getting angry.

"Because everything is too . . . I can't handle this profession anymore. I couldn't take it with you—the worry . . ."

"Susan, I'm getting out!" he said, grinning in relief. "As soon as the problem with Ross is settled. I don't want us to be looking over our shoulders for the rest of our lives."

She hesitated again, and it stung.

"You don't believe me again, do you?" he asked in astonishment.

"I . . . Remy, I'm just unsure of everything right now. Can you understand?"

"Sure," he muttered. But he was furious over her obtuseness. And *his* stupidity. He told himself this wasn't the time to ask her, but he couldn't help feeling that she was punishing him a little longer.

"Remy, please," she began earnestly. "You're an honorable man—"

A horn honking interrupted her. Lettice had pulled alongside their car and was waving from behind the wheel of a mid-size sedan—of bright cherry red.

"Dammit," Remy muttered when he saw the color.

"I better drive that one," Susan said, sliding toward the passenger door. "Her driving skills are about on par with a crash derby. Remy, don't be angry with me for wanting to wait."

He took a deep breath. "All right, *chère.*"

She nodded, then got out and slammed the door behind her. Once she was in the car, they took off, Remy in the lead. In the hours alone, he decided it hadn't been the right time to ask. He also decided he would ask again when this was over.

And he wouldn't take no for an answer.

Washington traffic was as horrendous as she remembered it.

Susan gazed around in delight as they stop-started, stop-started their way down the avenue. There were hordes of cars filled with hordes of people—a lovely mass of humanity from which they couldn't be removed without a major fuss.

She had managed a second and third wind, but her sleep-deprived body was telling her not to go for a fourth. Remy looked about ready to drop, and poor Lettice had already wilted in the backseat. Susan giggled at the pun.

"Don't be so disgustingly cheerful, *chère,*" Remy said. "We might have managed to sneak in through every suburb and third-rate road, but it ain't over until the last beignet's been dunked."

"I know," she said, and grinned anyway. "Still . . ."

He grinned in return. "Still . . ."

At least he wasn't angry with her, she thought gratefully. She had wanted so much to say yes to him. He was all she would ever want in a man. But she knew he wouldn't just leave the Company. Side effects from Ross were bound to occur, and his honor would demand he stay until they were resolved. Then he would stay on. His job had always been a commitment to honor within the Company. He would still be needed.

She didn't know if she could handle that.

"Ahh," Remy said, catching her attention. "The house is white, so this must be the place."

The home of the first family dominated the distant view on Pennsylvania Avenue. Susan laughed. "Side entrance, don't forget."

"I've sat down the street from it for many an hour in a parked car," he commented.

Nobody tried to stop them from reaching their goal. At the gatepost Remy gave their names to the guard. The young marine checked his list, made a telephone call, and after hanging up gave a dubious look at the two of them and Lettice just waking up in the backseat.

"I understand you work for a branch of security, sir," the guard said, leaning in the window. "I'm afraid you'll have to leave all weapons at the gate."

"We have none," Remy said.

"Weeeel," Lettice said. "I'm afraid I do."

"Grandmother!" Susan exclaimed as Remy shook his head.

"Somebody had to be thinking about protection," Lettice said, handing over her purse. "I got it in Boonsboro."

The guard didn't bat an eye as he opened the purse and removed a revolver. Susan groaned while Remy turned around and glared at her grandmother.

Lettice shrugged. "Well, you said you were no James Bond."

"Next time we go into hiding, *chère*, we leave her home," Remy said as the guard waved them on.

Relief washed through Susan as they drove down the interior drive. She leaned over and kissed Remy's cheek. "I think we just dunked that beignet."

"I hope it's a real one, because I'm starving," Lettice said.

A few moments later the office portico came into view. An older man, ramrod straight, was waiting for them.

"Miss Kitteridge?" he asked when Susan emerged from the car. She nodded, and he shook her hand. "I'm Ned Casper. I've been expecting you since yesterday. Your lovely aunt is worried."

"We had a few complications, sir," Remy said, helping Lettice out of the car.

"Mr. St. Jacques, isn't it? I have no doubt you brought the ladies through them admirably." The man smiled and shook Remy's hand, then turned to Lettice and actually bowed. "It is a great pleasure to meet you, Mrs. Kitteridge."

"And you, sir," Lettice said, taking his hand.

He led them into the mansion and down several hallways to a small, cramped office.

"We need more space," he said as he sat down behind the desk. "Sister Stephen tells me you have vital information about security."

Susan glanced at Remy. They knew only that Theodore Casper was a military adviser to the President; they knew nothing about his allegiances. Now was the time to have great judgment of people, and hers had never worked right from the first.

Remy shrugged. "He's got your aunt's seal of approval."

"And if she's wrong," Lettice said, "she'll have to answer to a higher authority. Me."

Susan nodded, but she felt better when Remy took her hand. Drawing in a deep breath, she told Casper everything, Remy picking up the story from his side. Ned Casper made no comment. He only sat with his hands folded on his small paunch and listened.

". . . and we left the rental at a hamburger stand and made our way in," Remy concluded. "No doubt you'll find the car still there, although I suspect the extra 'passenger' we had would be gone by now."

Casper nodded. "You've stumbled yourselves into a mess."

"That's why we brought it to you," Remy said.

The other man smiled tightly. "There are some of us in National Security who have had second thoughts about Mr. Mitchelson's abilities . . . and loyalties. We've had to be silent, however, because of the rivalry between the Company and our branch. But this news will prove unhappy for some others. If you'll excuse me . . ."

To Susan's astonishment, he got up and walked out of the room. She blinked, then stared at Remy's and Lettice's equally disbelieving faces.

"Now what?" she asked.

"Firing squad at ten paces?" Remy said.

"You should have let me keep the gun," Lettice muttered.

The door swung open and the three of them automatically rose to their feet when Casper reappeared.

"I'm sorry. I had to tell someone I'd be late for a meeting," Casper explained. "Unfortunately I anticipate one problem with what you've told me."

"No tangible proof," Remy said.

Casper smiled. "But we have the element of surprise, I believe. I'll need your further assistance."

Susan could feel Remy become very still, like a hunting dog sighting the prey. Her hopes faded. She had been afraid he was too committed, and now she was seeing it. Granted, Remy had a vested interest in following this through. But it was his eagerness that was dismaying. She loved him so much, but she was so tired. . . .

Casper smiled when nobody refused. "We'll have to push him into doing something foolish. Not an easy thing with Ross Mitchelson. You two have worked closely with him. What can we do?"

"You would have to capitalize on his every weakness to get him to incriminate himself," Remy said.

"Aren't you forgetting something?" Susan asked in a quelling tone. "Does Ross even have a weakness?"

"Ross has been greedy, *chère*," Remy said. "I think he might understand that in someone else."

"Like you and Susan?" Casper suggested.

Remy nodded. "One thing about Ross is that he loves to be the smart one who outwits the opposition, and he lets you know it. I think that could be handy. If we could play him along into thinking we're greedy and alone . . ."

"I believe I could arrange anything needed," Casper said. "One of the advantages of my job."

Susan smiled sadly in resignation as Remy and Ned Casper began to form a plan.

•   •   •

"So you've teamed up now."

Remy listened for subtle nuances, but Ross sounded calm, not at all rattled at receiving a telephone call from the "Disappearing Duo," as Lettice had dubbed them.

"I think we need to talk about that, don't you, Ross?" Remy asked, pulling Susan against him in the small telephone booth.

"I agree."

"Where?"

Susan smiled reassuringly, but he could see the worried look in her eyes. His arm was around her back in a tight embrace, and he rubbed her shoulders with his free hand. His heart welled with emotions. Lord, but he loved her. Never more than at this moment. He hated what was coming, and yet . . .

Susan rested her cheek on his chest and listened to the back and forth between him and Ross over the drop point for money. Finally a time and place were set, and Remy hung up.

"Midnight at the university," he said. "Let's go before they're on this booth like flies to honey."

Once they were down the street and away, she said, "You're too tired for this, Remy."

"There's no time to rest." He grinned, knowing his adrenaline was up. It would hold him through what he had to do and be enough, he hoped, to do it without a mistake. "Anyway, I couldn't sleep with you in bed with me."

"I might just hold you to that."

He stopped and kissed her soundly. "I hope so."

"I love you."

"I hope so," he repeated fervently as they began walking again. "Susan, I don't want you to go tonight—"

"No," she said firmly. "If you're going, then I'm going. Besides, I have the female lead in this play, don't I?"

"If something goes wrong . . . No, *chère*, I don't want you there."

"Remy—"

"No," he said vehemently. "I'm altering Casper's plan. You stay with your grandmother. That's final."

"We'll see," Susan said.

"No, we won't," Remy replied.

Still arguing, they stepped inside a department store and disappeared.

At ten o'clock that evening Susan opened the French doors and walked into Ross's living room. Remy was right behind her.

So much for the change in the plan, she thought as she waited for him to close the doors. She hadn't budged from her stance. Besides, she was part of the plan. The real one. Now all they had to do was play it just right.

She wondered if Ross had noticed the momentary loss of electric and telephone power about forty-five minutes earlier, when the lines had been turned off to cut his alarm system. Dead easy, the alarm expert had commented when he was through. She hoped he was right.

The foyer light was on, and she could hear faint sounds from a room beyond it.

"The study, I think," Remy whispered. "Let's hope he's surprised that we're early."

"And right on time," she whispered back, excitement tempered with caution rushing through her system.

She had refused to let Remy come alone, and at the time that had been her only reason for agreeing to this dangerous charade. But now she could feel the attraction of the business. It was already seducing her just as it had Remy.

She took his hand, and his fingers curled around hers, giving her a mix of signals. She couldn't sort out the love, care, reassurance, anticipation, coupled with a sudden odd surge of primitive want, so she sent them all back to him in return.

Hand in hand they strolled across the foyer and into the study as if they owned the place.

Ross looked up from the briefcase on his desk. Shock drained his face white for one instant. Papers were scattered across the desk and a wall safe was wide open. Susan smothered a rush of triumph. They had a long way to go before that.

"I'm afraid midnight at Georgetown University was just unacceptable," she said, wishing the rest of her was as calm as her voice. "Ten o'clock at your place was much better."

"Especially before you left town," Remy commented, staring pointedly at the briefcase. He let go of her hand. "I don't believe that's for us, *chère*."

"I expect not," she said sadly.

"What are you two talking about?" Ross asked, his voice a model of puzzlement.

"We didn't quite trust you, Ross," Remy said, "to keep our appointment. At least not in the way we set it up. So we decided to visit and have our chat."

"What chat?"

Susan glanced at Remy. "He's going to play a game."

Remy sighed. "I really do hate that."

She turned to Ross. "Do you remember Trevor's

party two months ago? I went out for a breath of
air . . . it was so stuffy inside. I saw you with
Senator Harvey's aide, Ross. More important, I
saw the money."

"And" Remy added, "I've been tracking a rumor
about top-level turned agents and a certain senator's aide. Susan and I put two and two together
and they added up to Ross Mitchelson."

"Nobody would believe it," Ross said. He stood
unmoving behind his desk.

"We're not so sure on that," Remy said.

Susan waved a hand. "I hate what you've done,
Ross, but once you were a good friend. I feel I owe
you something. So does Remy. That's why we're
here. We want this over with. We're willing to let
you go if you promise to get out of the country.
And stay out."

"This isn't like you, Susan," Ross said, closing
the briefcase.

"Yes, it is. I'm sick of this, sick of you and what
you've done." She kept her gaze steady on him,
playing her role to the hilt. "I can't take this business any longer, the constant tension and the
lying to everyone. I want a normal life again, and
neither Remy nor I want to be looking over our
shoulders forever. It horrifies me that you can be
a friend in one breath and a killer in the next.
You disgust me, Ross."

He merely raised an eyebrow, saying nothing.

"Face it, Ross," Remy added. "We're a big liabil-
ity. We know too much, and we can raise enough
doubt about you to cause an investigation. If
we disappear, that will cause an investigation too.
I think you already figured that out, and I think
you've been doing a little packing here to get out.
Especially before our midnight date."

"I wonder what would have happened at midnight at the university?" Susan murmured.

"Something not good, *chère,* I guarantee. But we've screwed things up for you again, Ross. You're not going to arrange a third accident for Susan, or a first for me. You're not quite as shrewd as you think. In fact, you've been pretty damn stupid from the beginning, especially putting me onto Susan. A three-year-old could have done better." He paused for a long moment. "However, I'm perfectly willing to make you shrewd again. For a price."

Susan turned to stare at Remy, shocked by his words. "Remy! What are you saying?"

He shrugged. "I'm saying that Ross can spare something for our generosity. You have money, Susan. I don't. And I think he's made it difficult for me to collect my salary from the Company. Unfortunately he won't be around to rectify that later. So he'll have to do it now. It's the perfect insurance. He can't say I took a bribe without incriminating himself. And I can't say he offered me one without doing the same."

"Remy, please, no," she whispered. "Don't do this. Your integrity—"

"The hell with my integrity," he said sharply, still keeping his gaze on Ross. "I'm more sick of this business than you'll ever know, and I'm entitled to some decent 'retirement' funds for keeping my mouth shut. Ross understands that, don't you, Ross?"

"I understand that you're trying to entrap me," Ross said, grinning smugly.

A gun appeared in Ross's hand, the movement so sure and quick that Susan almost didn't see it. She froze, waiting. Remy didn't move.

"A gun is hardly necessary, Ross," he said. "We're perfectly willing to negotiate."

"I think it's quite necessary," Ross said. "You're the stupid one, Remy, using clumsy, outdated police tactics like entrapment. You never could give that up, could you? Even if I were moved by your little 'retirement' speech, and I wasn't, I certainly wouldn't give you money in front of the lovely witness you've brought with you."

Susan forced herself to concentrate on the words, not the gun. "I'm a witness?"

"Didn't you tell her the game plan, Remy?" Ross asked. "I expect not. You always liked to play Lone Ranger."

Remy said nothing.

Ross gave a sarcastic laugh. "Do you think I don't know where you were today? The name of everyone who goes in and out of that side entrance is on my desk within hours. But I'm not nearly as stupid as you've anticipated. In fact, it will be a pleasure to show you how far off you are in your assessment. I have no doubt those idiots patted you on the head and sent you on your way. But knowing you, Remy, you didn't like the idea of others handling this. You wondered if they even would. You decided to flip your thumb at them and solve this all on your own. Walking into my house, bold as brass, as if the entire army were at your back is just your kind of bluff. You've done it before—that was how we met. Did you think I wouldn't remember? Remy St. Jacques, the hero of the day."

"What!" Susan exclaimed, rounding on Remy. "You said we were authorized to take him in! You said we were getting a backup—"

"Shut up!" Remy snapped.

Ross smiled evilly. "Remy, Remy, Remy. When will you learn that the novice will give the show away every time? Fortunately for me, you always were a novice and an idealist, Susan. Your kind is easy to manipulate. It wasn't hard to figure out why you left Washington so abruptly, you know. I put two and two together myself and came up with Trevor's party. Then when I saw the picture of you two in the *Post* last week, I decided it was time for action."

She cursed under her breath. He was dancing around this. It was time to push.

"Is that when you tried to kill the 'novice' twice, Ross?" she asked. "You missed both times."

"Yes. That was amazing. And also very frustrating, I assure you. And to think you were supposed to be the easier of the two. Unfortunately this third time will have to be the charm—for both of you. I know when to cut my losses. I knew when to do it with your husband when he began to panic . . ."

Susan could feel the hairs on her arms rise. Ross, in his gloating, was giving them more than they bargained for.

". . . Senator Harvey's aide is waiting with my last payment. He's another loss I'll have to cut. The damn fool insisted on open meetings, and now he'll have to pay. Oh, and I also know when to take care of a job myself."

His gun spat fire at the same moment Remy dove. Susan moved automatically, then stared as Ross grabbed his shoulder. His eyes wide in utter disbelief, he slowly fell to the floor. She looked down at the little revolver in her hand, its barrel still smoking. She dropped it, her entire body numb. Suddenly none of this was exciting anymore, only terrifying.

People flooded the room seconds too late.

"Remy," she whispered, her voice lost in the noise of shouted commands. She made her way to him, her body beginning to shake.

He sat up, blessedly whole. She threw herself into his arms, sobbing her gratitude and her grief. She had never had to use her training before—or in such a way. But if she hadn't, Remy would have been . . .

Holding her, he cursed her soundly. "Where the hell did you get that damn gun?"

"Grandmother . . ." She gulped back her weeping. "She got it back from the guard and insisted I take it. I almost didn't. Lord help me, but I almost didn't."

"It's okay, it's okay," he crooned, cradling her against his solid chest. "I love you. You were magnificent, and you scared the hell out of me. Never, ever do this again!"

She held on and vowed never to let go of him. "I love you. Please, Remy, never, ever do this again either."

"I promise." He kissed her lips, her cheeks, her jaw, her forehead, each caress another vow to her.

The noise in the room finally penetrated, interrupting them.

"Where the hell were you guys?" Remy demanded of their audience. She felt him reach inside his shirt and pull out the wire he was wearing. "We damn near got killed!"

"It went down so fast. Sorry," Ned Casper said. He patted both of them on the back. "But well done. He came over very clear and very incriminating."

"Ross gave me too much credit for acting alone," Remy said. "Right on cue. I may be cocky, but I'm not a fool."

Susan had had enough talk. She reached up and pulled his head down for her kiss.

Lettice was waiting for them when they arrived back in Casper's office. She enfolded both in her embrace and cried like a baby. That nearly shocked Susan as much as what they'd just been through.

"I'm so glad you're both okay," she sobbed out.

"Me too?" Remy asked.

"You especially."

Susan laughed. "I told you she liked you."

She was too exhausted to be tired. All she wanted was a bed and Remy holding her tightly. Tomorrow she would deal with the damage.

"Where's the nearest Hilton?" Remy asked, clearly having the same thought.

Lettice smiled and wiped away the last of her tears. "I renewed my acquaintance with the First Lady, you'll be happy to know. She has invited us to stay here."

Susan gasped. "Here!"

"But . . ." Remy began, then swallowed. "Well, we wouldn't want to disappoint the woman."

"It is bad form," Susan agreed.

"Do you want the room that's supposed to be haunted by Lincoln's ghost?" Lettice asked.

"Naaa," Remy said. "I'll be too busy trying to persuade Susan to marry me."

Susan grinned. "And I'll be too busy saying yes."

Epilogue

"Only your son would spit up all over his christening gown!"

"He's great, isn't he?"

Susan made a face as Remy grinned proudly at their firstborn. Young Robert St. Jacques gave his father a sloppy grin in return as Susan tried to change his diaper. She swore he was going to be as much trouble as his father.

"Uncle" James Farraday peered over her shoulder and asked, "Did he spit up on some little girl?"

Susan gaped at him. "No. It was me."

"Ah, then history is not repeating itself. By the way, Remy, Anne and I have a security problem we need to discuss with you."

Remy's eyes lighted with interest. "Whatever you need, friend."

Susan managed to get her son dressed in a clean outfit as she watched Remy talking with James. She had been worried that her family wouldn't be receptive to him, but all her cousins had acted as if he were one of them. And Remy was hardly intimidated by the Kitteridges. In fact, he had taken one look at her trust fund and decided to make his own.

Susan smiled. Dressed now in a three-piece suit that spoke of success and confidence, he was well on his way. He didn't need the outer armor, though. He was his own man. Her heart pounded heavily as she remembered how he had looked right before he'd put it on. Nobody looked sexier in briefs than Remy.

Still, the garb of success wasn't bad, she thought —especially when one has been fired. Ross Mitchelson had proved to be quite an embarrassment to the government in the end, in spite of efforts to keep everything quiet. The Company had been reorganized and she and Remy had been left out in the cold in a typical reaction to the whistle-blowers. She had never regretted it, and neither had Remy.

The security business they had founded wasn't quite the normal life she'd expected, though. Remembering a few incidents over the past two years, she admitted it had just the right touch of excitement at times. Certainly enough for her.

"*Chère*, James wants us to secure the transportation of his latest purchase." Remy chuckled. "The Derby winner. He's worried it could be stolen."

Susan lifted her son up and propped him on her shoulder. "If you burp all over this dress, you won't have any college tuition, buster. The security will be no problem—as long as we can get a baby-sitter for Robby."

James laughed while Remy eyed her sourly. She knew he wanted her to retire again. He might as well want the moon. The night they had gone after Ross had showed her that in some ways she was no more immune than he to their former profession. Anyway, she had no intention on missing out on the fun.

"Is my latest great-grandson ready?" Lettice asked, coming into the nursery. Susan's cousins, Ellen and Anne, followed behind their mutual grandmother. Joe, Ellen's husband, brought up the rear.

"We want pictures of the baby with Grandmother," Ellen said as Lettice took the infant.

"A portrait of yet another victim of her matchmaking," Joe quipped. Everyone laughed.

"I told you to run for the Canadian backwoods," Anne said to Susan.

Susan slipped her arms around Remy. She would always love the feel of his body. She loved him. He had only to look at her and she knew she was loved in return . . . and desired. She swore sometimes that he was trying to make it up to her for falling asleep in that special "hotel" the night they'd caught Ross. That was fine with her. Remy's actions spoke for him in all ways.

She shrugged in true Gallic fashion. "It could have been worse. He could have gotten away in his Aston-Martin."

"I'm no James Bond, remember," Remy said, giving her an intimate smile.

"You're much better," she murmured back.

He kissed her, their lips clinging for a long moment.

"See?" Lettice said. "I knew what I was doing."

Susan turned in her husband's arms and faced her family. "Thank goodness there are no more granddaughters for her scheming."

"Agreed," Ellen and Anne said together.

"There may be no more granddaughters," Lettice said, "but my work is hardly done." She paused, then added with great satisfaction, "You're forgetting I also have grandsons."

Everyone in the room gasped in horror.

Lettice smiled.

THE EDITOR'S CORNER

It's been a while since we acknowledged and thanked the many people here at Bantam who work so hard to make our LOVESWEPTs the best they can be. Aside from our small editorial staff, members of the art department, managing editorial department, production, sales, and marketing departments, to name a few, all contribute their expertise to the project. The department whose input is most apparent to you, the reader, is that of our art department, so I'd like to mention them briefly this month.

Getting the cover art exactly right isn't an easy task. No two people ever envision the characers the same way—and think of how many people read our books! Our art director, Beverly Leung, knows how important it is for you to have a beautiful cover to look at. Her job starts by commissioning an artist for a particular book. The artist is given a description sheet prepared by the author herself. After models who most closely resemble the characters are selected, a photographic shoot is done, and from those photos the artist/illustrator creates first a sketch and finally a painting for the cover.

During the entire process Beverly works to ensure we—and ultimately you—are pleased with the finished artwork. She's done a fabulous job since taking on the assignment, and it's reflected in the gorgeous covers we're able to bring you. Thanks, Beverly.

Now on to the good stuff! Next month's LOVESWEPTs feature heroes so yummy, anyone on a diet should beware!

Kay Hooper weaves another magical web around you with **THROUGH THE LOOKING GLASS**, LOVESWEPT #408, the next in her *Once Upon a Time . . .* series. Financial wizard Gideon Hughes fully intends to shut down the carnival he had inherited. But when he arrives to check it out, he's instantly enchanted by manager Maggie Durant—and balance sheets loose all interest for him. Gideon is intrigued and unnerved by Maggie's forthrightness, but something compels him to explore the deep and strange feelings she stirs in him. Then Maggie openly declares her love for Gideon and in so doing, lays claim to his heart. Amid clowns, gypsies, and magicians, Gideon and the silver-haired siren find the most wondrous love—and together they create their own Wonderland.

In **PRIVATE EYES**, LOVESWEPT #409, Charlotte Hughes delivers the kind of story you ask for most often—one that combines lighthearted humor with powerful emotion. Private investigator Jack Sloan resents being asked to train his

(continued)

partner's niece, Ashley Rogers. He takes one look at her and decides she doesn't belong on an undercover assignment, she belongs in a man's arms—preferably in his. But he soon discovers he's underestimated the lovely single mother of two. Ashley works harder than he ever imagined, and her desire to win his approval tugs at his heart—a heart he thought had long ago gone numb. Charlotte puts these two engaging characters in some hilarious situations—and also in some intimate ones. Don't miss this very entertaining romance!

Sandra Chastain often focuses on people living in small towns, and her knack for capturing the essence of a community and the importance of belonging really makes her books special. In **RUN WILD WITH ME**, LOVESWEPT #410, Sandra brings together a wicked-looking cowboy, and a feisty lady law officer. Andrea Fleming has spent her life in Arcadia, Georgia, and she's convinced it's where she belongs. Her one attempt to break away had ended in heartache and disaster. Sam Farley is a stranger in a town that doesn't take kindly to outsiders. He doesn't understand how someone can have ties to a place—until he falls for Andrea. She makes the handsome wanderer crave what he's never known. This is a touching, emotional love story of two lost people who find their true soul mates.

Deborah Smith's heroes are never lacking in good looks or virility—and the hero of **HONEY AND SMOKE**, LOVESWEPT #411, is no exception. Ex-marine Max Templeton could have walked off the cover of *Soldier of Fortune* magazine. But when he encounters Betty Quint in a dark mountain cave, he finds in her one worthy adversary. Betty is a city girl who has moved back to the town of her ancestors to return to the basics and run a small catering business and restaurant. She can't believe the man beneath the camouflage and khaki is also the local justice of the peace! Of course, there's no peace for her once Max invades her life. But Betty is looking for commitment. She has dreams of marriage and family, and Max runs his wedding chapel as if it's all in fun—and with the knowledge that marriage is definitely not for him. You'll love being along for the ride as Betty convinces Max to believe in a perfect future, and Max proves to Betty that Rambo has a heart!

Doris Parmett has a lot of fun inventing her wonderful heroes and heroines and researching her stories. For her latest book she visited a local cable television station and had a great time. She was asked to appear on a talk show,

(continued)

and it went so well, they invited her back. Absorbing as much atmosphere and information as she could, Doris returned to work and created the love story we'll bring you next month. In **OFF LIMITS**, LOVESWEPT #412, Joe Michaels and Liz Davis make television screens melt with their weekly hit show. But off camera, Liz fights to keep things all business. Joe refuses to deny the sexual tension that sizzles between them and vows to prove to the vulnerable woman behind the glamorous image that a man can be trusted, that their life together would be no soap opera. These two characters produce a whirlwind of passionate emotion that sweeps the reader along!

What woman hasn't fantasized about being pursued by a ruggedly gorgeous man? Well, in **BLUE DALTON**, LOVESWEPT #413 by Glenna McReynolds, our heroine, Blue, finds the experience exhausting when tracker Walker Evans stalks her into the Rockies. Blue is after the treasure she believes her father left to her alone, and Walker thinks his is the valid claim. When Walker captures her, she can't help but succumb to wild sensation and has no choice but to share the search. Confused by the strength of her desire for Walker, she tries to outsmart him—but her plan backfires along with her vow not to love him. Only Glenna can blend exciting elements of adventure so successfully with the poignant and heartfelt elements that make a story a true romance. Don't miss this unique book!

We're pleased and proud to feature a devoted LOVESWEPT reader from down under as our Fan of the Month for June. Isn't it wonderful to know stories of love and romance are treasured and enjoyed throughout the world!

Hope your summer is filled with great reading pleasures. Sincerely,

Susann Brailey

Susann Brailey
Editor
LOVESWEPT
Bantam Books
666 Fifth Avenue
New York, NY 10103

FAN OF THE MONTH

Wilma Stubbs

It gives me great pleasure to represent the Australian fans of the LOVESWEPT series, and there are many as evidenced by the fact that one has to be early to get titles by favorite authors such as Kay Hooper, Barbara Boswell, etc.

I have been reading LOVESWEPTs since early 1984 when the Australian publisher distributed a booklet comprised of excerpts from the first titles. I was hooked—and impatient! So I wrote a plaintive letter to New York for a publication date, and the nice people there sent back a letter full of information.

As the mother of two semi-adults with their associated interests and friends, and the wife of a man who has worked shift work for twenty-five years, I've always found romantic fiction to be my favorite retreat. LOVESWEPTs cover a broad range of moods—from the sensuousness of Sandra Brown to the humor of Billie Green to the depth of Mary Kay McComas to the imaginativeness of Iris Johansen, particularly her Clanad series with the delightful touch of mystique.

I have often recommended to troubled friends that they read some of the above authors in order to gain a balance to their lives. It seems to refresh one's spirits to dip into other lives and gain a better perspective on one's own.

60 Minutes to a Better, More Beautiful You!

Now it's easier than ever to awaken your sensuality, stay slim forever—even make yourself irresistible. With Bantam's bestselling subliminal audio tapes, you're only 60 minutes away from a better, more beautiful you!

__	45004-2	**Slim Forever**	$8.95
__	45112-X	**Awaken Your Sensuality**	$7.95
__	45035-2	**Stop Smoking Forever**	$8.95
__	45130-8	**Develop Your Intuition**	$7.95
__	45022-0	**Positively Change Your Life**	$8.95
__	45154-5	**Get What You Want**	$7.95
__	45041-7	**Stress Free Forever**	$8.95
__	45106-5	**Get a Good Night's Sleep**	$7.95
__	45094-8	**Improve Your Concentration**	$7.95
__	45172-3	**Develop A Perfect Memory**	$8.95

THE LATEST IN BOOKS
AND AUDIO CASSETTES

Paperbacks ────────────────────────